A CITY ON A HILL

– an indirect memoir –

stanley jenkins

Outpost19 | San Francisco
outpost19.com

Copyright 2013 by Stanley Jenkins.
Published 2013 by Outpost19.

Jenkins, Stanley
        A City on a Hill / Stanley Jenkins
        ISBN 9781937402433 (pbk)
        ISBN 9781937402440 (ebook)

Library of Congress Locator Number: 2001012345

OUTPOST
    19

PROVOCATIVE READING
SAN FRANCISCO
NEW YORK
OUTPOST19.COM

Acknowledgements

"As We Approach (After Babel)" originally appeared in *32 Pages*.

"Beyond the Piney Wood" originally appeared in *The Oyster Boy Review*.

Parts of "George" originally appeared in *The Salt River Review*.

All other work in this volume originally appeared, in some form or another, in *Eclectica Magazine*.

To Mary, Tom Dooley,
and all the good patrons of Cafe Blue.

A City on a Hill

(An Indirect Memoir)

Stanley Jenkins

"A city set on a hill cannot be hid."
Matthew 5:14 NRSV

"The light shines in the darkness,
and the darkness did not overcome it."
John 1:5 NRSV

As We Approach (After Babel)

On my American plains I feel the struggling afflictions
Endur'd by roots that writhe their arms into the nether deep
—William Blake

Tell. What shall I tell? Tell of the conflict of passion and security from a long time ago. I went fishing with my Dad once. The knife in cold water. And the liquid smear of red. Do you remember the snake? Long and black. Curved like the ripples. It snatches the guts and is gone.

Clean the fish and sing old songs.

Michigan. The land has gone elsewhere. This is what I was thinking from my window seat at the back of the bus. I wasn't thinking about my father or my new life in New York, or even about cancer or the fact that this time my father would surely die. I was thinking about Michigan and its expressionless face, as tender and as taunting as an autistic child's.

Meanwhile, in Howell my father's body was transforming itself into a vast network of darkening tumors—"melanomas" they are called. He was turning black from the outside in as if already his body were returning to dirt. I imagined soy beans and field corn cropping up between his ribs and joints.

When my aunt called, I boarded the bus at Port Authority. I hadn't been back in seven years—in fact, since I'd left home for college in the Northern Ohio flatlands.

Consider for a moment the problem of origins. How can it be that we come from one place and not another? My people were all shiftless wanderers before they settled in Howell. No landowners these folk, but all second and third sons and daughters without birthright. A rootless nation, and yet something drew them here to this place. Between Lansing and Detroit, in the center of a right hand's palm, which has neither love nor life lines—a fortuneteller's nightmare.

My father's face was lost to me on the bus, but I could still see the rest of him in my mind, rocking on the porch, his back to the land, his face to the house, chin slightly lifted, hands empty. Rock. Rock. Rock. And me in the yard watching, and behind me the stupid emptiness of Howell, and beyond that a presence, an awareness. Watching. Watching. Watching.

But on the bus. Word disease.

But on the bus. The telling. The re-telling. This is the story. To tell, to re-tell, to re-member the limbs that were broken when Babel first fell: Return.

But on the bus I was thinking about Michigan, and I was thinking about a face beneath a mask and other things which invisibly distend smooth surfaces. Michelangelo's slaves yearning for escape from marble prisons. I was returning.

And old songs.

Out of the cradle endlessly rock… rock… rocking / a reminiscence sing…

That from Walt Whitman.

J. Calvin Biggs. It's a signed name, but it's mine. And in time it comes to identify something immanent but ineffable. My mother named me after her own grandfather, John Calvin, deacon in the Presbyterian Church and vicious-faced corn liquor dealer who would not take his wife to see the doctor and who would not acknowledge her fits until at last she had to have a hysterectomy—because in Howell in those days an old woman's fear and epilepsy were the result of a wandering womb. "Hysteria," they called it. Papa, I called him. He lived a long time, and then he died. They gave me his name.

I grew up in Howell, Michigan, roughly in the middle of the state between Lansing and Detroit. Home of a former Grand Wizard of the KKK, and in the outskirts, strange utopian communities of rabid NRA and State's Rights devotees. The people here are fundamentally the product of an American religious impulse, but a mutant impulse: a Spirit turned violent and moving across the face of the swamp. Those damned Yankees moving from their Vermont and New York farms, their eyes heavy-lidded with Puritan dreams of the City on the Hill—and later the effluvia from the Canal Boom washed ashore like an oceanic tide pool far from the Great Lakes—and still later the mass exodus from the forever carpetbagger South and from dead Appala-

3

chian hills—these people, my people, came here and went no further. It's as if the land itself has gone to sleep. The dreams make us crazy out here.

I grew up in the house on the hill in Howell. Civil War heroes lived there before me. My father was an important man in town. President of the Rotary Club. I had a name, a history, a place in Howell. I wanted more. A future.

Bury my body Lord, I don't care where—say / Bury my body Lord, I don't care where—say / Bury my body cause my soul is going to live with God / O yeah.

But on the bus. Partial memory. And so the beginnings of return and the re-covering of the original face. Tell. What shall I tell? Tell of sad Enkidu and of standing in proud Gilgamesh's shadow. Remember. I remembered. Paula Cassiday. She came to Howell from suburban Detroit when I was a senior in high school. She'd run away three times, and her parents felt that the quietness and stability of a small town would take away her restlessness. She wore patchouli oil, smoked clove cigarettes, had frizzy hair, and knew things she'd never learned from TV. It was between her thighs and on the back of a silent Michigan landscape that I first learned the possibility of being other than who I was.

"Do you want a cigarette?"

"I don't smoke."

She smiled at me.

"How do you know? Have you ever tried?"

One Friday night in the early fall, Paula borrowed

her father's car, picked me up from the house on the hill, where my own father sat rocking and drinking in silence, and took me out here to this faceless Michigan swampland. She sat me down next to a dead tree, and I could smell her hair, and my shoulders were trembling though the night was warm.

"You're afraid of me, aren't you?"

I didn't say anything.

"I thought you were different."

"Different from what?"

She smiled.

"Why don't you kiss me?"

Her thighs beneath her faded jeans, her breasts beneath her evergreen sweater, the touch of her palm scandalizing my knee, moving closer—cars on icy curves—moving closer—I tasted her tongue.

"See, that wasn't so bad, was it?"

I couldn't catch my breath.

"Just relax Calvin—people do it all the time."

"What if you get pregnant?"

"I'm on the pill."

She sat watching me.

"Haven't you ever wanted to just say fuck it all and go for it, Calvin?"

I nodded.

She lay down beside me. She unsnapped her jeans and spread her legs. Her underwear was white and glowing in the moon. I touched her breast. Her lips were warm. She sighed, and I lay with her. The night was cool on my bare legs, and her back was arched. Remember. I remember.

Howell. And as we approach. I wanted more.

Tell. What shall I tell? Tell of exile in the city and stage repetitions. Tell of the new life in the land east of Eden. Remember. I remembered. Every weekend in New York, the lights would come up on a stage empty except for me in a chair with my cowboy hat down over my eyes. It was always the same. The truly American myth of the lone gun. Authority and lawlessness with a badge. I was the sheriff.

On stage in the city I did not think of my origins. I had no origins. Mime, my chosen medium, was perfect for avoidance—a void dance where white-faced ghosts walked against invisible winds in highly stylized gestures. And I too was merely myth in my white-out face—the archetypal loner in my chair. Perhaps I was aging—perhaps I was the original aging shootist waiting for that new young gun who would take me out to make a name for himself. A notch on a pistol belt. Marcel Marceau does Shane.

The lights would come up on me alone on stage. This was my showcase. In the troupe I was the slapstick artist, the Buster-Keaton-faced silent movie star. There is something about my face which allows for the humor of expressionlessness. The lack of response to all stage-calamities.

Christie would enter at this point, whooping wildly and silently and riding her mime horse. Among all the members of the troupe, she was the purest mime. Her life on and off stage was a subversive myna-birding of established forms. She kept stealing the grant money to buy drugs. Not for herself, of course, but to pass them out on the streets. With an eruption, she would enter and shatter the silence and the pathos of the lone gun. She was the loose cannon, wild one, shooting up the town—and I was the tired and sadly inadequate lawman.

The humor was conventional. My horse would not stand still for my mounting. I could not draw my gun without shooting myself in the foot. We raced through the stage town, a Marx Brothers version of "Gunfight at the OK Corral." And I, the tired and once proud hero of the American West, milked laughter through incompetence and stone-faced resolution.

But of course, the piece ended with me bringing the outlaw to justice, and of course, it ended with me back in my chair, a reclining figure. Christie, the wild one, was subdued—for the moment.

Remember. I remember. High Noon.

J. Calvin Biggs. I left Howell. After college in the Northern Ohio flatlands, I came to New York. The denial of origins itself. New York is the city of bad consciences and expatriates. I was a mime in the city. But as we approach and on the bus: Return. I was on the bus, and I was returning. Memory. It's the embodiment of loss and impermanence, but still the Theseus thread leading home. You should have seen me among my fine fellow travelers. American pilgrims. There is a restlessness in our America, as if a whole nation were overtired and unable to relinquish itself to sleep.

Memory and word disease. Motion. Everyone on the bus was going home. Going through the motions of a habitual Homestead Act.

And as we approach. Tell. What shall I tell? Tell of the wound and of the need for masks. The garden.

"Dad?"

We're at the bottom of the hill now in the backyard. The garden.

"Dad?"

A small plot. Radishes. Tomatoes. Cucumbers.

"Dad?"

Imagine now the father before the fall. Limbs like mountain roots, trunk rising to the heavens, piercing the clouds' veil. On these shoulders rest the sky's beams, beneath these feet the ocean's bottom. American Atlas. But do you remember learning that every ring in a tree's trunk represents a year? And do you remember realizing that you had to cut down the tree to count the rings? My father.

"Dad? Are you alright? What's wrong? Dad?"

Clutching at his chest now. Dropping his hoe. His face. Twitch. Twitch. Twitch. And a word tries to be born in his mouth. "D-d-d-d-d. D-d-d-d-d." I'm standing there. I'm feeling things. I'm trying to run to him. I'm appalled. Twitch. Twitch. Twitch. And a word. He's down. He's breathing hard. Eyes rolling wildly. The fall. And beyond, an awareness. Watching. Watching. Watching. Horse and rider into the sea.

My father had a minor stroke when he was forty-one years old. There was little permanent damage, a slight paralysis of the face, and speech was difficult. Word disease. I guess I took it seriously. These things, too. My sad America. A strange literalness. We were going to be the Shining City on the Hill. Every night my father sat on the porch, every light in the house lit, his back to the land, his hands empty. Rock. Rock. Rock. Out of the cradle endlessly rock…

…rock-a-my soul in the bosom of Abraham/Rock-a my soul in the bosom of Abraham/Rock-a my soul in the bosom of Abraham/O rock-a my soul.

Just like an old song.

I wanted more. And as we approach.

I wanted more and more and more. What good is a history and a home if it's a judgment? There was college, education, and the promise of a thousand delights if I would only dare to demand that they be there. To dream and to want to be more than you are. That's the American birthright, isn't it? I created myself anew and became a stranger to Howell. I denied the sentence of origins and Babel. ("Haven't you ever wanted to just say fuck it all and go for it?") Desire.

"Getting a little too big for your britches, I would say," my father would offer in his slurring slow-speech.

Those were hard times for us then. My father sullen and withdrawn; my mother, so curiously the absent woman in my memory—the missing womb—she sewed in her room and watched "Laverne and Shirley" on a portable set, her jaw clenching more firmly with each stitch. I read forbidden books and learned to build escape ladders from rubblewords. I was above it all. He is rising.

"Don't think you're too big for me to whip you, young man, and I'll do it, too, if you don't watch that mouth of yours." Slur. Slur. Slur-slow-speech. And me all the time watching his mouth and flexing my tongue and growing deft of speech. I will not stumble and stutter and start and stop. Taunt taunt tease tease tease please Daddy please speak speak speak. Rock. Strange flowers grow in the silence. Your face is frozen. Old songs.

Lead me, Jesus, lead me/Why don't you lead me in the middle of the air/And if my wings should fail me/Won't you buy me another pair.

Tell. What shall I tell? Tell of Icarus flights and Daedalus dreams. And as we approach. But still on the bus. We shall return. Behind the firehouse and beyond the abandoned railroad tracks—even then the trains refused to run through Howell. St. Clare's.

I did not know then, because Catholics and Protestants did not share their mysteries, but it had been a seminary at one time, dedicated to St. Francis of Assisi's spiritual consort. Clare, the clear one. I did not know the inner algebra of the myriad orders or the charters or names of the religious of Howell. For me it was a sad and forgotten garden. Weeds grew in the porticos. Sad, somnambulant, stone statutes stood like pillars of salt—don't look back—surrounded by milkweed and dented beer cans. This was my first theater, my first stage, among the headless Madonnas and Risen Lords with broken lilies. Far, far from the Vatican—my own St. Damiano's.

And strange, strange hagiographies.

One day when Francis went out to meditate in the fields, he walked beside the church of San Damiano, which was threatening to collapse because of extreme age. Inspired by the Spirit, he went inside to pray. Prostrate before an image of the Crucified, he was filled with no little consolation as he prayed. While his tear-filled eyes were gazing at the Lord's cross, he heard with his bodily ears a voice coming from the cross, telling him three times: "Francis, go and repair my house which, as you see, is falling completely into ruin."

—St. Bonaventure, *The Life of St. Francis*

Repair my house.

You see, that was still before the fall. I would run down the hill full tilt, arms revolving, a giant turned into a windmill. I would dash into streets without looking. I would bark back at dogs. I would sing radio songs. I would run and run and run until I reached Clare, the clear one. And there. Wild plays and melodramas with me as the perpetual lead. Solemn ritual theater. And the sparrows were my audience.

I don't know if this is peculiar. I think that most children must act out the plays of their age. Cowboys and Indians. Cops and Robbers. War games. I did silly vaudeville routines that I half-invented, half-stole from the Charlie Chaplin shorts my mother rented from the Helen Plum Public Library on rainy Mondays in July. The tramp. God's little poor man. Poverello. Joculare. I did not know then that my silent-movie hero was the American reincarnation of Francis, dead saint and brother to me. This would have to wait for college in the Northern Ohio flatlands. But we are getting ahead of ourselves. Now our America is littered with the remains of the religions of our ancestors. Scratch the surface, and saints and prophets crop up. (Behold: Archetypal Mormons say lost tribes of Israel here—and Jesus too!) But I did not know that then. For me, it was a secluded stage, an arena in which to play. Clare. The clear one.

And so the beginning of the dream of imagination even before the fall—though I did not understand this at the time. To re-create, to re-present, to re-member: Repair the house. There is healing and reconstruction in our plays. To live your life as if it were a movie, as if it were silver-screened and larger than life. J. Calvin Biggs. Or so the promise goes.

But you are not finished. Tell. What shall I tell? Resume the tale of wings as of eagles and the revelation of recognition borne aloft. Another stage in a far, far city. The city. New York. The piece has ended. The lights have come down, and I am supposed to leave the stage. I sit in my American slouch chair.

"Calvin." Stage whispers. "What the fuck are you doing?"

I am sitting.

"Calvin."

This is the part I don't like to tell. Sluggish slur slow speech.

"Calvin."

I am sitting.

In the darkness of a completed piece, in the anticipation of the next sketch.

Christie comes back now silently, and she takes my hand. And she leads me gently. And I cannot talk because I have five holy holes in my body now and there are plants growing out of my flesh. And I can see soy beans and field corn. And I am leaking rich rich loamy loamy soil soil. I am above it all. Strange flowers grow in the silence.

On stage in New York, I had an anxiety attack. I'd heard of it happening to others. The heart. Pounding. The inability to move. Panic. Your face is frozen. I couldn't move. Struck. Stroke. Strike. And beyond. Watchingwatchingwatching. Behind stage in Christie's lawless arms, I trembled. Return to land. Earth. Howell. Icarus, the land is calling. Bury my body in the bosom of Father Abraham.

J. Calvin Biggs. And as we approach. These things, too. To tell the story and to redeem what is lost in memory. Imagination. It's the canopy and the silver screen over the vast expanses—gaps perhaps themselves the result of the glaciers that gouged out the face of this land so long ago. But on the bus I was still waiting for the fullness of the vision to come round. Beatific. And Jefferson's dream. You should have seen me. The sin is not in wanting too much. (Is it?) It's just that you have to return to purify the eyes. But on the bus, I believe. I think I believe. And as we approach. My lips are unclean. A fiery coal, Lord. Me and Isaiah.

A word that cleans.

Northern Ohio flatlands. Cleveland. Elyria. The industrial north is like a vast graveyard for weight-lifting equipment. Back in Michigan in the seventies, there were bumper stickers on foreign-made cars that said, "Last one out of Detroit, please turn out the lights." And in Cleveland, the river burns. America pumped herself up in these regions and then left. Who killed Lake Erie?

But out here also are the Amish. Ohio. They still raise barns. Still ride horse and buggy-ed into town. Still scrape clods from their shoes at the back porch. Our America will never be a rural Eden again, but the rubble from the original walls remains. Impossible, perhaps. Reactionary, perhaps. But still. Who will wake up the land? Strengthen what remains. Re-member.

Finney College is out here as well. Named after Charles Grandison Finney, the greatest of the nineteenth century revivalists. They say he nearly single-handedly set Western New York a-blaze. The Burned Over District. Scorched earth. Well, that is, him and the Holy Ghost. And his college in the undeveloped lands of the Midwest was a utopian experiment of sorts. Utopia—from the Greek, *ou topos*, meaning literally "no place." And I guess Finney, Ohio, is about the closest to "no place" you can get anymore. But the mandate, the destiny, the will, and the call to transform the world into a fiery blaze of Love and Justice: all that still remains out there amidst the closed auto plants and steel mills. It's like a little piece of the Old Testament among a late-coming people. Those who have always already exodused. After Babel, the pilgrim's long hard climb to Pentecost. Tongues as of fire.

On the bus as we approach, I had to change in Cleveland. All told it takes about eighteen hours from New York to Lansing. Greyhound doesn't stop in Howell anymore, and you have to change again in Detroit. Travel. You can't get there from here. In the station, waiting to go, still occupied with the hidden face of Michigan and my father rockrockrock, I remembered Ohio.

Tell. What shall I tell? Tell of the advent of black snakes and adult cancers in the dream. Remember. I remembered. Aia Caldwell. She was in my Intro to Drama class, wore purple laces in her shoes and white cotton dresses. She was Desdemona to my Othello in the scene we prepared for class.

Iago. In our rivers. And in the white streams of our coupling.

"Calvin?"

I am standing.

"Calvin? What are you doing?"

I am standing.

Tappan Square with the memorial arch, monument to American missionaries killed in the Boxer Rebellion. It's night now.

"Aren't you going to say anything?"

I can't talk. My face is frozen.

She is crying now.

"What are we going to do?"

My face is frozen.

And then the sudden vision of serpents winding writhing arms into the nether deep. My American plains. Like eels. Like black worms. Like grasping, clutching, yearning, wantwantwant desire arms, and they are encircling the nethernether of my lovely Aia.

"I am so sorry."

Her eyes flashing now to meet mine.

"You fucker!" She's hitting, pummel, pound, my flush face—we are both ashamed. To know that there are consequences. "What are you sorry about?" Pummel my face. Hit me. And I will know your outrage, your feline Kali scream in the insensate Chaplin bones of my face. "What are you sorry about?"

"I don't know." I am not lifting my arms to defend my face. Her fury. She is sobbing deep in her breasts that will leak Mamamilk and stain her white cotton dresses before the serpent's squeeze. "I don't know."

We both know.

"I am pregnant."

Afterwards. Tell. What shall I tell? Tell of the silence imposed and the fiery sword of shame blocking off all return. Mimes in America. My mute American Messiah. My new bus was ready to continue its journey. Resume. Redeem what is lost and remember what is broken. Home to Howell, and learn what must be forgiven. And what must be forgotten. From my bus I see the soil rising. And Jefferson's vision. I see too much. Milkweed.

But you are not finished. Tell. What shall I tell? The old bodily nightmare. Resurrection in the garden. I am ten years old. My Mom and Dad. Good people. I am at the kitchen table. Why after all these years?

"Calvin?"

"Yes."

"You are so quiet."

It's Mom. She's good people. Fecund soil—ripe ripe—things grow good in our garden.

"Do you want to talk about it?"

"Why didn't you tell me before?"

"Oh Calvin." Sadly shaking her head. "We didn't want..."

"Want what?"

I am very nearly livid. Things grow good in that garden. Bad crop I guess. Could have been me.

And later that night, Mom and Dad in bed now. Sleeping maybe. And I am awake and at the window. Watching. Watching. Watching. Francis grow good. I am at the window. Watch. Could have been me. The garden. And the moon shows me the soy beans and the field corn from the fields. Francis lives with the worm. Things grow down there, too, you know. Calvin, you are so quiet.

When I was ten years old my mother told me of my older brother, Francis. Original mime. Born dead. Stillborn. Buried thirteen years, and yet things grow so good in our garden in Howell. I did not sleep for weeks. Soy beans and field corn. Return. I am leaking loamy loamy. Papa, great-grandfather, you took away Mama's great-grandmotherly womb, and I am J. Calvin soil soil Biggs. Should have been me. Worms down there, too, you know. Leaky loam loam. He will come back and take what is his. He is rising!

And when we changed again in Detroit, I had a sandwich wrapped in cellophane from the machine because I was very hungry and it is hard work remembering and knowing and being healed, and maybe I don't want to do this anymore because sometimes it's better notknowingnotcaringnotseeing. The face of. But as we approach and on the bus. Judgment and Howell.

J. Calvin Biggs. Memories and dreams. Like all the broken pieces, and if you could only put them together again. Humpty Dumpty. I grew up in Howell, Michigan—roughly in the middle of the state. My father's face was hidden and paralyzed. I played in abandoned seminaries. Gardens everywhere in my Michigan with their promise of ripeness and return—but now only separation and exile. Speech lost to the mime. And what about my saintbrother, Francis of Assisi-on-the-Howell? These things, too. A place for everything. A home, if we only have the courage. And desire is the snake thread that holds it all together.

Haven't you ever wanted to just say fuck it all and go for it?

And again. On the bus there is the curious sensation that you have always been approaching this point and that all that has gone before has been the dramatic pretext, the plot, the excuse to do what must be done. Return. The Kingdom is at hand! Redemption. Recollection. Sing the old songs again. The only ones that matter. On the bus we tell the stories that have always been told. Babble on after Babylon. Rock. Rock. Rock. Endlessly, my sad America. End.

In New York I had come to the realization that a future without roots was like that magic herb of immortality that proud Gilgamesh found then and lost now and forever. Do you know that story? It has always been told. We tell it here, and we tell it there. Tell. What shall I tell? Tell of the man who knew everything, of Gilgamesh the Babylonian king. Brave warrior. Statesman. Two thirds divine, one mortal. Conqueror of all things but death. Remember. I remembered.

"Gilgamesh?"

He is sitting.

"Gilgamesh?"

It's the primordial waters. We're in the boat. Dusk now. He has descended and returned, his great beard dripping. His empty hand stretched out over the waters. Trembling. Trembling. Trembling.

"Gilgamesh? It is getting dark. We should go now."

Trembling. Trembling. Trembling.

And the ghost memory of the serpent rising out of the waters and the snatched magic.

"Gilgamesh..."

"Hush."

"But..."

"Hush."

As the sun sets, the shadows over the water grow long.

My sad Gilgamesh. To the very ends of the earth he traveled to find the magic plant that would replenish all that was lost. Eternal Youth. Immortality. Ponce de Leon looked for it here in our America. To never die. Be new again always. And so here in the very center of the world, in the middle of the ancient waters, the brave king descended. Plunge, plosh, plash. Sink. Sink. Sink. And there at the very bottom. The magic herb.

Heart pound. Lungs to burst. Air swollen in the head. He surfaces! Sputter, sputter, sputter. To always be born again. He has the magic. And now he is in the boat, and now he is exulting, broad chest and arms like branches. Proud, proud, brave Gilgamesh.

But then, silent, contoured like the waves themselves. The black snake. The hand of Gilgamesh stretched across the waters. Furious now, magnificent—though so sad to say, so sad to say—the serpent snatches away the magic, snatches it from his hand, now and forever, and returns with it to the abyss. Loss. Separation. Return to earth. Ripped from its roots the magic must die, and so too dreams and visions and hopes and ecstatic verities until we all become mere-mimes, mere-ghosts, mimic, mimic, mimic. A void dance. End.

But now. Begin. Speak. Tell. Remember. I remember. (Is the sin in wanting too much or in not having the courage of your desires?) I was going home. Find out what must be forgiven. And what must be forgotten. (I believe. Only sometimes I can't get the words right.) The snake. (Must we learn to love the snakes also?) Desire kills. Desire gives life.

Howell. I wanted more. But in New York I learned that you had to go back before you could go on. Return again. Howell. Raise the dead. My sad sad dead dead Enkidubrother sleeps in your cold ground. He will come again. He is rising! Return. Repeat until it must be true.

Just like an old song.

Michigan. The land has gone elsewhere. This is what I was thinking from my window seat at the back of the bus. I could no longer recall my father's face. Only the image of him rocking and rocking on the porch. His back to the land. His face to the house. Every light lit now and the doorway itself glowing. Soon he would get up, walk across the porch and cross the threshold. And on the other side. And as we approach.

Will the circle be unbroken? / By and by, Lord, by and by / There's a better home a-waitin' / In the sky, Lord, in the sky.

On the bus it struck me stroke strike for the first time that my father was really going to die. Not a TV death or a shrinking black circle closing on my beloved Chaplin walking into the sunset—fade to black. But the unmentionable. Ineffable. Privates. Down, down:

So high can't get over it / So low can't get under it / So wide can't get 'round it / O rock-a my soul.

It was like forgetting your own name and realizing that nothing changes. After Babel words don't touch anything. But then again, after Babel some words are just too beautiful to say. They must become flesh.

I was looking for the complete sentence. Good grammar. Christmas on Earth.

And as we approach. How ironic. The bus itself broke down. Route 96, between Detroit and Lansing. (Vernacular—not yet sacred tongue: Oh 'bout eighty miles as the crow flies. Hour and a half. Sumpthin like that. But she blew just this side of D-19. We didn't get no further than Howell.) How ironic. You see, Greyhound doesn't stop in Howell anymore. You have to go all the way to Lansing—East Lansing actually, home of Michigan State—and Malcolm X used to walk these roads here about, too, don't forget. You have to go right past the exit and then doubleback, like a snaky switchback climbing some western mountain range, though in this case, more properly some Ararat or maybe Sinai. You can't get there from here.

The bus broke down. Sudden silence. The queer sensation of coming up from air after a deep deep plunge, or maybe waking up. Stillness. After the long long motion and hum of forward movement, it seems almost obscene. Stop. I could smell the highway weeds and the hot pavement. "Sorry folks. Looks like we got a little delay. We got another bus comin' out for us though." And me now standing up. Backpack hanging on one shoulder. And down the aisle toward the door. "Sit down son—I can't let anybody off." And me standing there looking out through the door, closed now. "Look, I'm sorry but you're going to have to sit down. It's the law." And me just looking. Not at the driver. But that autistic face, drawn close now so you can hear its inner hum. The land is taking a journey, too. We're all going home. "Are you going to sit down or what?" I'm standing. Behind me I can hear him getting up. A hand on my shoulder. Then for no reason at all. Maybe he remembers something. His hand to the handle. The door opens, and I step out onto the ground earth soil soil of my Michigan origins. The driver. I don't even look back. But he's watching me as I wade through the high high highway weeds of the embankment. The door closes.

Tell. What shall I tell? Tell of the ancient story. The only story possible after Babel. Security and passion. Garden and snakes. These parts are broken. Who will recombine them, if only for a little while? And I saw an army of ghosts, of long lost saints, Kings or Queens in their own day, some of them the dead authors of books that still live. And they were building a huge telescope from the rubble that lays strewn across this sleeping land. Words as bricks. Kabbalistic associations as mortar—and the lense? Only partly a mirror. (Funny thing. Somehow when we're not looking, the myths become personal.) I walked across the sleeping wolverine face of my Michigan. Home to Howell. More ancient ritual theater now to complete the pattern then anything else. Home. Our pilgrim-strides in this America. I think of the Sioux warriors and their Ghost Dance:

All Indians must dance, everywhere, keep on dancing. Pretty soon in next spring Great Spirit come. He bring back game of every kind. The game be thick everywhere. All dead Indians come back and live again. Old blind Indian see again and get young and have fine time. When Great Spirit comes this way, then all the Indians go to the mountains, high up away from whites. Whites can't hurt Indians then.

—Wovoka, the Paiute Messiah

Broken arrow-words become flesh and dancing dancing dancing. Until Great Spirit come and make these dry bones live. Redemption. It's an old story. The only story. After Babel every word bears the muddy, divine fingerprint. Tell. Dance. Walk. With every movement we try to reconstruct our tower. I believe. Someday. Someday. Any day now.

My sad America. Wounded Knee. All dead now. And what must be forgiven. And what must be forgotten.

And so as I approached Howell, I had a choice. Consider for a moment the problem of pattern. If we know the fulfillment. If we know how the story ends. Is it best to continue, or to make up "new" rebel stories with the hope that they might escape the totalitarian pattern? Again. Reformulate the problem. How do we escape origins? Tragedy? And in the attempt do we become rootless, non-non-non not there entities? In the sky, Lord, in the sky? You should have seen me on stage in New York—all mime and myth—yet ultimately ultimately ghost self condemned to haunt the same old stories over and over. And this return. Wasn't it an attempt to go only so far? To acquiesce to the pattern with hopes that at the final moment. The Rosetta Stone? The original Ur-language? The original face re-covered like Jubilee in Old Testament testament—revealed like that magic coin in the magician's hand? Tell and tell again until it must be true. Impossible possibility.

Tell now. What shall I tell? Tell of new patterns. Not Nietzsche's unfettered unloved cold cold careening world—open sea of possibilities like Kerouac on his jaunts across our country only to end up fat bloated bitter John Bircher drunk. Dead. Dead. Dead. (This must be the John Calvin in me. The fear of chaos. The unwillingness to live without patterns. 'Cause nihilism, cousin, nihilism. You can't undo what has been done.) (But then again. Maybe. To a void. Only repeat. Endlessly?) I think of my father now, his back to the land. No. Just say yes. And him standing up and entering that house of lights and then gone gone like Francis. Like Gilgamesh. Like Orpheus' wife forever. Yes. And I will follow. And I will cross the threshold, too. Though ineffable. Speechless. Nameless. And I will create re-create new patterns in embracing the old. I believe / I don't believe. Unio Mystica / Exile. Scattered across the face of the earth. Children of Adam. Progeny of Eve. Allialliallcomefree.

After Babel: Pentecost. I will turn again in the doorway and face the face of the land. Again. I shall return. Singing new hymns with tongues as of fire.

"Francis. I guess I didn't really expect to see you."

"Well, you know how it is."

"I see you've got your silent movie star costume on."

"When in Rome..."

"I've been meaning to ask you... I mean... Do you think he'll recognize me? I've changed a lot since I left."

"I know. I know. Tell me about it."

"Well?"

"Hard to say, Cal."

We walk together a while in silence. Him duck-waddle jerky like the cameraman can't keep a steady hand.

"Want to know something funny? I was always afraid when I was little that you were going to come back and—well, I guess I thought you'd be really pissed, because I lived and you didn't."

"What's so funny about that?"

I couldn't think of anything to say. Then:

"I used to play in this old seminary, you know, and

it was called St. Clare's, and I guess that was supposed to be your "friend" or whatever you'd call it. I never cleaned it up. It was all ruined. I thought about it. I thought I should clear the weeds or something. But I never did. I just played there. I didn't even know about you then but..." I'm crying now suddenly. Hoping he'd tell me that my plays, my Chaplin dramas, my vaudeville routines were enough. "I should've tried to make it better."

Francis didn't say anything.

"I'm really scared. Daddy's dying."

Still no response.

"Francis?"

He's gone.

Mumble, mumble, me as I walk through golden meadow hair—on my way home—like a refrain in some song. Again and again and again. Crying renewal tears.

I entered Howell alone and saw the house on the hill alone and moved across the street alone and through the yard alone and climbed the hill alone. We live as we dream.

"Calvin? I've got something for you."

Smell of soil and soy beans and field corn and grease paint.

Michigan.

Behind me. Though I do not look. Face. Original face. All my Americas.

"Calvin?"

A baby. Newborn. Playing with a snake. Laughing. Laughing. Laughing. And beautiful beautiful herbs and roots in the snake's mouth. Laugh. Baby. Laugh. Laugh. Laugh. Desire kills / Desire gives life.

Home.

Without knocking I turn the knob. Go through the door, and am swallowed in the house of lights. J. Calvin Biggs. Endlessly end. Home. Gone.

Again.

The Binding of Isaac

*Behold, the fire and the wood; but where is a lamb for
the burnt offering?*
—Genesis 22:7

Snow on the mountain. A thicket trembling in the
wind. The brittle crackling of twig against ice. Around
the bush the snow is broken and trampled.

There is a clearing. There is a fire. And in the clearing, the smoke and fire consume the carefully constructed pyre. The day is gray. In their struggle, the
man and the boy are cloaked. The knife alone, gleams.

Hands grope and reach for thick handfuls of the
coarse wool. Legs are thrashing, breath is visible. The
boy is sweating.

"Hold him!"

"I can't"

"Father..."

The black bone handle of the knife presses firmly into the palm of the father's hand. The cool metal
dances in the smoke. The boy struggles to hold horns
and neck twisted and bound in the crumpling snow.
Behind them the fire convulses heavenward.

"Father..."

The thin blade pressed against the neck. The muscles
in the father's arm tighten, the grip clenched. Press-
ing downward, he can hear the whimper of the ram.
Wool snaps beneath the blade. Eyes are rolling, expos-

ing pink-gray lids. The smoke mingles with the breath of all three. A quick lunge and the flesh is ripped. The blade disappears or bends as if it has been dipped into a puddle.

"Father..."

Snow on the mountain. Father and son standing together. The old man looks away, the boy directly into the fire. The melting snow hisses. The boy begins to sweat in the heat.

Snow on the mountain.

"How much farther?"

"Not much."

"The wood is heavy, and my hands are cold."

"We are almost there."

The old man walks a few steps ahead of the boy. In one hand he carries the bowl of fire, in the other, the knife. The flame creeps over the edge, fanned by the wind, reaching out toward the long folds of his cloak. The boy struggles to keep up with him.

"How will we know when we get there?"

The snow crunches beneath their feet as it is broken up, and the perfect whiteness of the landscape is scarred.

"The clearing lies just beyond."

"Father..."

"Hush, child."

The boy shifts the wood in his aching arms. They walk in silence, the wind beating at their exposed flesh and swirling the flames about the rim of the bowl.

Legs are thrashing, the blood throbs and gurgles around the blade. It is thick and dark, staining the snow, hissing and steaming as it boils out over the matted wool. His hands are covered and seem to melt under the tide of red. The knife is removed. The snorting slows, the gurgling hushes. Legs are still.

Father and son walk together in the snow. The boy trails a few steps behind, struggling to keep up. His small feet, thickly wrapped, dart in and out of the white sea. A dull ache starts at the small of his back and proceeds into his thin arms. His nose is running.

The old man walks steadily, looking straight ahead. He grips the knife tightly. The metal gleams, scattering sharp light fragments across the unbroken whiteness. The flame leaps frantically from the bowl. In the distance is a small clearing surrounded by harsh black rocks and scraggily bushes. The climb has been gradual but begins to increase now as they come closer to the rocks.

"Is this the place, Father?"

"This is the place."

"Will we rest a while before we get there?"

Snow on the mountain. The ram lies still. Eyes are rolled upward. The troubled snow around them is pink. They stand together, the old man looking away, the boy directly into the fire.

"We cannot rest yet."

The boy nods, trying to ignore the sting of the wind and the ache of his burden. They walk together silently, the wind absorbing all sound in its howl. The flame licks at the father's long cloak. The knife gleams.

"Father..."

"Hush child."

Each log is placed precisely where it needs to be to sustain the flame. The kindling has been carefully laid in the center, the snow scooped away by bare hands. All is ready. The wind rustles through a thicket. The crackling of twig on ice. The old man stands motionless, staring into the bowl of fire. The boy looks away.

"Father..."

"Hush child."

"But where is the lamb?"

The old man reaches into the bowl and pulls out a firebrand. He stands up slowly and turns to face the carefully constructed pile of wood. He does not look at his son.

Snow on the mountain. A thicket trembling in the wind. The brittle crackling of twig on ice. An arm is tautly extended to its full length, at the end of which a knife trembles. The blade is poised. All is still. Muscles strain, veins strain.

Father and son stand together. The old man looks away, the boy directly into the fire. Quietly, his arms begin to rise, stretching out. The flames leap upward, ripping at the sky, lashing the cold whiteness. Slowly, he turns. The old man looks away. Slowly the boy turns, his arms open wide.

All is still. The father looks up at his raised hand, held in suspension. His eyes follow the length of the arm and reach the hand, resting on the blade. The tension mounts, the restraint is waning, the muscles stretch as if they will snap. Eyes are closed. The tension breaks. The knife released like an arrow. Down. Down. Eyes are closed.

Abraham looks away. The boy begins to turn faster and faster before the flame, his arms outstretched. Slowly, his feet leave the ground, and he spins faster and faster. As the flame shrieks and dances hysterically, he is rising. Isaac is rising. Snow on the mountain.

Setting the Woods on Fire
(Dancing With the Devil)

[Click....]

OK? Ready. Testing 1,2,3. Testing 1,2,3.

Here goes.

In 1958 my father killed ten people in the course of eleven days. They made movies about him. They wrote songs. He was executed by the state of Nebraska a year and a half later. He was 18 years old.

Popular character in American imagination.

I grew up outside of Chicago and Kansas City. I, of course, never knew my father. I had a normal childhood. I had a suburban childhood. But my adoptive parents made a decision early on to tell me all the facts. I don't know if they made a good decision. They don't either.

When I was in college, I read an essay by Friedrich Nietzsche. It was about History. It's been years since I've read it. But I remember that he said that at certain points a culture's History becomes paralyzing. The way to a present, then—the way to a present—is by way of forgetting. To forget is to create a new world, to clear a space for a present, to clear a space against the high-tide-rising of ages.

I am an American. A clearing.

Are we still recording?

I

O my baby—you, who say you love me.

You said you wanted to hear. To hear it all. And I expect I'm bound to tell it. Tell it all. How is a man to keep the old blood from rising? How is a man to walk barefoot and bleeding in Babel-lands—O for to find the balm of Gilead!— when the devil knows his name? That's the story, baby.

Listen. I've been drinking. But we've got to talk. Clear the air. Make a clearing. Figure this thing out. Got to tell it. The whole story. And from the beginning. I'm drunk. But still...

Bopbopaluaawhopbamboo!

Crank it up!

Listen baby, after my father was electrocuted in the chair and he jerked about like a young Elvis in heat in 1958 and the Nebraska State Prison yard was crowded with hoods and juvenile delinquents in chinos who cheered and chanted my father's name like a movie star—after that had happened, I tried to grow up.

Which is to say, I grew up in small towns that were no longer small towns. Those were the days of white flight, you understand. And subdivisions were creeping out and swallowing up the small towns. It was worse in the seventies. But this is the sixties we're talking about. And it was bad enough. Late sixties. When America tried to enjoy itself. When America tried to still be a kid. Man, we were born old! Youth culture. A band in every garage. When Puritan America found out that it wasn't good at playing at all. Man, we were just too damn serious. Even ecstasy got mandated—like the bombs of the Weatherman Underground. Land of the grim. Ever seen a subdivision?

Now don't get me wrong. I understand the suburbs—and what they meant to a whole generation. Hell, I grew up there. I imagine Teds and Alices all over the country newly married after the war—and we're talking the fifties here now—moving out of their parents' houses—and I can just see them using their GI loans and GI bills—and Ted putting on a tie to go to work just like his Daddy never did before him except on Sunday mornings for church when everybody knew he would just as soon not be there (and anyways would likely as not slip out the back before the sermon was half over and smoke a filterless Camel or Lucky Strike with his foot up on the running board of an ancient Model T), and I imagine these Teds and Alices buying their first homes and losing regional accents and, you know, just being real proud about that.

This is something I truly understand. I'm proud of them myself, these countless Teds and Alices. These people without roots. My people. Blood.

But they got lonely out there, I think. Ted and Alice. In the suburbs. And they had their kids. And Ted kept getting those promotions. And Alice, she had every new appliance that came out. But man—I can see them out there, and they weren't happy.

Yeah. I remember that. I remember things. Hell, I remember things that happened before I was born. So let me tell you like it is. We-e-e-e-el-l-l-l-ahellahella... And baby it ain't no lie, the latter half of the twentieth century has been the latter half of the American Century. We are a Rock'n'roll nation. And History and beaucoup Authoritative Texts tell us that Americans have enjoyed a measure of success unparalleled. And the weird thing is that our America has never learned to enjoy itself.

Do you remember what my father said when they finally caught up with him and he had killed at least ten people and they asked him if he was sorry?

"Well," he said, "at least for a little while, me and my gal—we had us some fun."

This is not bullshit. This is not just me avoiding the issue at hand. There is a rage and a sense of vengeance in our entertainments. Don't you think? Contents under pressure. I know you think Elvis was just a whiteboy stealing from black folks—and God knows that was true—but Elvis was something else, too. I'll tell you a secret: America vented its anger in Elvis. America raged. America screamed. And those cheers coming from the crowd at the Pan Pacific Auditorium in Hollywood in 1958 (and don't kid yourself, baby— that was after he'd made his first movie and supposedly got domesticated) were howls from something dark.

Something real old.

And it only got uglier.

But back then, in 1958, it was the several-story-high flames of a silver refinery smokestack seen from miles away in the Arizona desert at night, and you were frightened and fascinated. American Gehenna. Old Faithful! "Thar she blows!"

Like I said, in 1958 my father killed ten people in eleven days.

Old blood.

Blah. Blah. Blah. I got angles. I got stories. A million stories. Man, you got to clear a space just to breathe. Gotta get a purchase on this thing. We tell each other stories. History. The stories are the walls, the dyke, the levee. And anyway you said you wanted to hear it all.

O my baby. It is strange to say, but I have always seen my life to be emblematic. Something about my family, and I'm talking here about both my families. Yeah. Two fathers. My Daddy, he's out there running through the woods—"Run through the jungle! Don't look back!"—he's running, a ghost always riding lost trains—"I hear that lonesome whistle blow"—huddled over campfires, murdering folks in their sleep, desperate, a strange lack of restraint, a howl, vicious, feral, vital. Ever smelt the sweetness of rotting leaves? And the other. I got two Daddys. My adoptive father. You know he was never really much of a farmer. In fact, his people weren't even from Nebraska. Hadn't ever lived in Nebraska—that was my adoptive mother's people. At the time of my adoption, my folks had long since made that great divide. You know it stirs a whole lot of things up when a man exchanges his workshirt for a suit and tie.

Originally his people were from Oklahoma. Wildcatters. Or at least they heard the call when that dark, rich oil burst from the barrens. Saw the light. My father's people saw the light, and they raised themselves. Raised themselves until my father was able to attend college (I kid you not—God bless the GI bill!), and so he was stepping up in our America. And my first father, well of course, they never met, but my first father, I think maybe someday—O my Baby—I fear sometimes at night, when I hear what cannot be the screech of an owl, cannot be because I live in the city—when I hear that sound—O my baby—I think maybe that he is coming for me. Drag me back. Pull me down. Bury me deep in this soil—this curse. And I wanted my new father to protect me. I wanted a new father.

And that is probably why I got religion. I told you about that. I was sixteen. It was no surprise. Religion was one of the things my people brought with them after they crossed the great divide and my father became management.

I remember two things. I remember my adoptive mother's mother. Her face flush and furious. Terrified. She had just slapped my adoptive mother. "Don't you ever think that you're better than us!" My adoptive mother in tears. She had just shown her mother her brand new sewing machine. A fine machine. She was so proud. And a hand reaches out and beats her down.

And the other thing I remember. I remember prayer meeting at the Bethany Methodist Church. Wherever we went—we moved so often in our upward flight—there was a Bethany Methodist Church. I remember prayer meeting. And my mother's people had been Free Will Baptist. And prayer meeting. And suddenly my mother's face got twisted, and words were gushing out like vomit, and she was speaking in tongues and so ashamed. So ashamed. Her past would not free her.

But me. I never had a real present—always caught up in a past. So I had no problem returning to a legacy my people struggled so hard to leave behind. I understand things discarded. O Sweet Jesus!—I fell upon my knees, and I'm telling you my love, my sweet, I felt him. Him. Holy Spirit! And I went limp. O slain in the Spirit. And perhaps you've seen it on TV. I was dancing. Dancing. Dancing.

See, baby. I know the power of love. Don't think I don't. I have seen with mine own eyes. The coming of the glory of the Lord. I was sanctified. And my Daddy—my banshee-beastie-evil Daddy—was dead. Dead. Dead.

Blood memory.

Seven weeks before my father went on his killing spree, he held up a gas station in Lincoln, Nebraska, with a shotgun. There was an attendant and a young woman. My father saw them together when he held the gun and demanded quick obedience. He emptied the cash register, and then he took the attendant and his young woman to the car. He told them to get in. In those days you did not need to drive far to leave the city far behind. They parked out there in the Great Plains with the city lights calling them. And then my father tied up the attendant and made him watch as he raped the young woman. When he was done, he put the barrel in the attendant's face and fired.

But old things return. Like the sap of a tree in spring—blood memory.

And the young woman was left out there. After she was raped, she was left out there. And after the sound of the shot wasn't ringing anymore, she was left out there. She screamed and screamed. She was found dazed and wandering beyond the city limits at dawn.

Her parents never reported it. And her people took care of it. And she was pregnant. So she was sent somewhere else to have the baby, and when she came back, an older relative was prepared to take on the child. And so she gave the child to the relative. And the child was raised by the relative.

Baby, it is the dark secret of America. You cannot escape your origins. Someday, you gotta pay the fiddler.

And I grew up in the suburbs outside of Chicago and Kansas City. Trying not to think about the blood of the fathers. Raised by good people. Relatives of my Mama. Good people. Trying to find stories that might keep the high muddy water at bay. Trying to stay afloat.

Got a million stories, baby. Got a million stories. And my hands ain't clean.

I have held my father's hand.

Drunken jibberish? I don't know.

How long have we known each other now, baby? It's been awhile. Hasn't it? Look at me. I'm 41 years old and never been married. And now you say you love me and want to spend your life with me. Now you say you don't care about the past, or where I come from, or who my Daddy was. You love me.

Well, that's just fine. And that's a good thing. But I gotta tell ya, it unnerves me, baby.

It's like I'm standing on a cliff. And I'm gonna jump. And you still believe we're capable of walking on air. Don't get me wrong. I'm gonna jump. But before I jump, I've gotta talk and talk and talk and tell you my name. My stories. There is space in the stories. In the telling of the stories. So I got drunk, baby. And I'm drunk now. And I got a hold of this tape recorder. And I'm talking to you. In the voices of my people. In broken English. In fragments. Da-do-ran-ran.

On January 21, 1958, my father was visiting his girl-friend. She was fourteen years old. He was seventeen. Her breasts were only beginning to bud. Her parents did not approve of my father. He was short and bow-legged and carried a rifle. He was Elvis in your living room. And they were a God-fearing couple and beat their daughter when she needed it. And they told my father to leave, and he picked up his rifle and shot the father. Then he moved the gun across many inches and shot the mother. And they were silent. And they weren't telling him anymore that he was hanging around too much. But the little sister. She was two years old. The little sister wasn't quiet. And so my father stuck the barrel of the gun down her throat. And she was choking. And then he fired. She was quiet then. And when he looked up, my father's girlfriend was watching TV.

Old blood.

II

Alright. I flipped the tape over.
Check this out. More stories. History. High muddy.

My adoptive parents never laid a hand on me. Never struck me in anger. They treated me as one of their own, and my three older sisters insisted upon drawing me into their games. They dressed me up in old dresses and once introduced me to my mother as a new friend, a new little girl just moved into the neighborhood. And my mother. She was so sweet, my baby. She extended her hand and said "Welcome."

That night I sat through dinner with barrettes in my hair. I had lipstick on my face. And my sisters were giggling. But I was treated as an honored guest at the table. I was so proud. And when I went to bed, scrubbed and PJ-ed, my mother told me she was happy to see me again. Told me she had missed me.

I have always loved her for that. She is a woman who knows how to let a man be something else for a while. I expect she knows a thing or two about longing. About neither being able to return nor to be fully where she is.

Anyway. O my baby. When my adoptive father died about ten years ago, I did not call. I have not spoken to my sisters since. I never went home. My mother is out there. I never even called her.

And me. Out here in the big city. Such a city. City of lights! New York is the city of make-believe. No one ever seems to have grown up here. No one here ever seems to be who they used to be.

After my adoptive father died, I changed my phone number. Unlisted.

I smashed every plate in the house. I ripped up every book I loved. I pushed a pen into the palm of my hand until I drew blood.

I woke in a cold sweat to a ringing phone.

I stood before the bathroom mirror stupid in rage. Clenched. Tremble. Tremble. Tremble.

Gave a karate kick to the image in the mirror. Hunka-hunka burning love. Thumbs up sign.

Went to the movies at 84th and Broadway.

Listen, baby. My father and his girlfriend stayed in the house with the bodies of her family for six days. They put a sign on the door. "Stay a Way. Every Body is Sick With the Flu." People came to the door, but they were not let in. Then my father and his girlfriend left. In the winterlight my father saw things disappear in the rearview mirror. And they rode out into "that vast obscurity beyond the city, where the dark fields of the republic rolled on under the night." And the next day they got stuck in the January mud of a farmer's field.

The farmer came to them. My father shot him in the chest, and then he shot the farmer's dog when it stood before him without complaint or hope. It was time to go.

So my father and his girlfriend left the car and bodies behind. And they walked to the highway. And there they stuck out their thumbs. On the Road. They were maybe thinking to light out for the territories. And somebody in America was thinking, "I first met Dean not long after my wife and I split up." And then pausing, and then more thoughts: "I had just gotten over a serious illness that I won't bother to talk about, except that it had something to do with the miserably weary split-up and my feeling that everything was dead."

And wouldn't you know. The high school sweethearts stopped for them. He was 17 and she was sixteen. So my father got the drop on them and told them to drive. And they drove out into lost land until they came to an abandoned school. And a settlement that was no longer there. And ghost houses. And went down down into the cellar of the abandoned school. And my father shot Romeo six times in the face. And Juliet. After she was dead, someone stabbed at her genitals with a knife. My father later said that it had been his girlfriend. She was a jealous type. They did not stop but dashed out again into dark night in the car stolen from the sweethearts. And they were singing.

> *From heart-break some people have suffered;*
> *From weariness some people have died;*
> *But take it all in all,*
> *Our troubles are small*
> *Till we get like Bonnie and Clyde.*
> —Bonnie Parker, 1934

III

Man! What was going on back then? This is old. Older than memory, baby. I imagine an ancestor. An ancestor and a ghost. It must be the 1850's. The ancestor is an American type. The type you might imagine hollow-eyed and shattered in a bar. One more lost soul along the Lost Highway.

But the bar part's not right. He does not drink. He does not not drink out of some sense of propriety or even because he never thinks to drink, but because of a kind of a meanness, a kind of perverse continence, an aggressive refusal to extend. He is a town drunkard who refuses to drink. A fool who refuses his part. The ancestor. He is like what you'd imagine a black hole is right before it becomes a black hole: a sun, a star, an explosion so concentrated upon itself that it passes into its opposite, so concentrated upon itself that it collapses and passes through the looking-glass—except this sun, this star, this implosion is frozen on the lip of collapse. A smashed fly on a mirror, touching the place where both worlds meet. A door never opened or closed. A meanness. A refusal. A vengeance.

Timothy McVeigh.

I imagine this abstemious ancestor, and how he would have been a farmer, and how he would have hated and feared the land.

They write books and songs and you see movies about farmers, about how connected they feel to the land. Banks come with bulldozers and are met by farmers with guns. "You can take my machinery, but you ain't getting my land."

But I've never met a farmer who, in certain weather, wouldn't tell another story—a story they live in their nightmares. A story about the fear and hatred. The resentment toward the land—its otherness, its indifference, its maddening tolerance of us. There is a haunting out here.

My ancestor would have been a little more straightforward than his neighbors. His life would have been a kind of constant presentation, a witness to this fear and hatred. With every step behind the plow he would have reminded his neighbors of the truth of their dreams, their nightmares. He would not have been a popular man.

Jeremiah among the beseiged.

And the ghost. I imagine an ancestor.

O my baby. This is what I'm saying: there are things that you can never know about a man. Things you couldn't even begin to explain. And so maybe it's best to just keep quiet about what you can't explain. But this is what I'm saying. O my baby. In the silence I hear other voices. Many voices. And these voices are neither not my own nor entirely unfamiliar. And this is what frightens me.

When the talk gets too broken. Fragments. And it is like cold water now rising up in the cracks. Ice floes. And I am frightened and drunk.

This is what I'm saying. Baby.

So it's an ancestor I imagine. And a ghost. I imagine the time is the 1850's or so. He would have come over in the potato famine. He would have seen people he knew with children with bloated bellies. He would have seen his own. But it's nearly ten years later, and he's been here nearly all ten of those years. And he has been prosperous in America. You can see him. You can see him in other people's old family daguerreotypes. Common ancestor. American type.

But one night in the 1850's, the ancestor does something uncommon. He does something really bad, baby. He drinks the water from a hollow log when the moon is full. And this is not good. This is not good at all.

The Indians used to have stories about the spirits who walked the land. They told of angry and hungry ghosts enraged by the refusal of the whiteman to see them, to acknowledge them, to give them fear. But the whitemen did not see the spirits, and now was the time of the vengeance of the unseen. Fear would no longer be enough.

And so, drinking from a hollow log when the moon was full in the American wilderness in the 1850's—such deliberate superstition! such courting of the spirits which no whiteman must see—and so, doing so when it was the time of the Mechanic and the Common Man and the Great Democracy and the Abolitionists in places like Philadelphia and Concord, and there were still utopian communities throughout the Burnt Over District in New York State—O a shining city on the hill cannot be hid!—was not good. It was not a good thing to do. Traitorous. And evil must had to have come of it. And spirits walked these lands even after President Jackson evacuated the Cherokee along a trail of tears and so many died that there could never be a remembering of names and we should have no truck with them, and yet still these spirits whispered dark truths in the ears of pilgrims and poor wayfaring strangers.

And there was great cause to give fear to the spirits. But it was too late, baby. The spirits wanted only vengeance. And sometimes good men lost their reason in the woods and rutted about in the moist moist soil, hungry to discharge.

But mostly the ancestor that I imagine would stand silently. Silent as a daguerreotype. A reproach. A witness. There is a meanness in a man's heart. There is a need to lash out. A need to no longer be bent and beaten, to no longer be cringing, no longer be in need of tenderness. And this need is in the heart of the ancestor, and he is waiting. He is waiting. Across ages. Like a cancer. Waiting with the spirits. He knows that he will

49

not always be so silent. He has drunk the water from the hollow log when the moon was full. And he has given fear to the spirits. He is intoxicated.

This is what I'm saying.
Old blood.

And so sometimes I would like wake up and I'd be really giving it to her, you know. And then I'd see these hands and they're all sticky and red—like you stuck 'em in a can a paint but it's not paint—and so there I'd be really going at it and her beneath me like a little rolly polly—her nubby little bubbies sloshin' around—and those hands, and it's the old in and out, in and out, you know? but this time it's a knife. And I don't know whose hands those are.

Jesus!

It ain't no knife. Cuz she was with me later when we took out the shoe salesman.

So anyways. We took off, man, didn't leave nothing for the laws. Just left the sweethearts down there in that cellar like couple of tulip bulbs—and we planted em, that's for sure. So me and my gal we took off roaring and hooting, and we weren't going nowhere in particular and couldn't get nowhere in particular and so came back to Lincoln. You know, I'm always coming back to Lincoln. Can't ever get away from Lincoln. And we pulled up to the bigwig house—man those fatcats! Jesus H. Christ! You talk about your Mansion on the Hill!

That Hank Williams is somethin' else.

So anyways. Walked right in like we fucking owned the place, and the shotgun didn't feel right. Made me a little nervy. It just didn't feel right, you know?—and I got all hepped up, so this time I just stuck her with a knife. Stuck her with a knife. She was fat, too. Big fat old rich lady. Had to push. And her fat bubbling out all over the place made this like farting noise—and that was pretty good—and I got the giggles and leaned over and told my gal to pull my finger, but she was in a mood like her time of the month—and so I just put a little elbow grease into it and got her done. And did she squeal? Whoowee!

Gurgle gurgle! Cuz I had to slit the bitch's throat. And she just kinda caved and plopped like when you smash an old rotten pumpkin.

And then there was the colored girl maid—and that don't really count—but she had a pair on her let me tell ya. And my gal, well she must a seen the way I was looking at her, and she just turned away, and I could tell she was getting a head up, so I did her real quick—nothin' special you understand, just did her like that and didn't do the other, you know? But I kinda wanted to, you know?—anyway just stuck her, and she didn't make any noise and that was kinda cool, cuz then it was like there wasn't any noise at all, and I got the chills, and it was like I was watching myself in a movie. And there I was. Man! Big as Jimmy Dean in Giant—and I was just 2 cool 4 words, and digging it. I looked great, man, and I don't know why I was up there on the screen—but you know how you get, sitting in a dark theater and the movie you're watchin' is real gone, and it's like there ain't no space between you and the guy up there you're watching, like you're just the same, but the distance is still there—it just seems like it don't really matter? Well that's what it was like. I was watching myself do her and thinking how great I looked, and there was distance between me and the guy up there doing those things—I mean like real distance, like you could feel a breeze blowing between us—but the distance hardly mattered, and so I did her, and it felt real good like I was real big or sumpthin', and she didn't make any sound at all until I like woke up and heard that little rat dog yapping at me and reached down and wrung the little cunt's neck cuz there just ain't time enough for that—just ain't time enough.

Is there room for this too, baby? This voice, too? I hear it when I'm not talking. I don't mean all crazy like. You know what I mean. I hear it in our America. The keening of blood in veins. The ancestor intoxicated.

And I am drunk.

There is more. Things you ought to know.

Oh my baby. There is something old in our America. Something very old. Older than the stars. When I was sixteen, I got religion. I wanted to be someone new. I wanted to be new. "Whoever is in Christ Jesus, there is a new creation." That's what I wanted, baby.

Oh and when I was sixteen, I got it. I got what I wanted. You've heard the stories. You've heard the tales.

But I have not told you everything. When I was sixteen I got something else. Something I can't shake. I wanted the gift of tongues. Possession. Tongues as of fire. I knew that it was not good to wish for things not given. I knew that. But I wanted the gift of tongues. I wanted to lay down my burden—Oh study war no more!—to lay down and open my mouth, wanted to speak the words that would come, the beautiful, meaningless words, words of pure sound, words of pure rhythm. Tongues of angels. That's what I wanted.

And I prayed. And a presence came to the end of my bed. And it sat at the end of my bed. But it was not good.

Baby. It was not good.

> *I've got to keep movin'*
> *blues fallin' down like hail...*
> *And the days keeps on worryin' me*
> *there's a hellhound on my trail*
> —Robert Johnson

IV

And then the real fatcat himself came home. And I met him at the door with the gun. "Welcome home, Daddy." And then I blew him away.

And me and her. Well we just lit out again. Took the sumbitch's limousine. God damn right! Mother fuckin' Mansion on the Hill. And we're driving, see? Driving like bats out of hell. Hellhound on our trail. O do not lay your hand upon the head of Cain to harm him or to hurt him. We are marked, my pretties. We are marked.

And we lit out, and don't you know they had 200 of
them laws sitting there in a roadblock. Nebraska National Guard. Two hundred of them motherfuckers.
And I am howling now. Gasping great chunks of air,
and there is spittle in the corners of my mouth. And
we are in Wyoming now. And we are hot, I'm telling
you. Had to make the switch on that car and I don't
mean maybe. So what do you think? Just then we pull
up upon the shoe salesman sleeping in his car. Poor
bastard shoulda stayed awake, cuz tonight I am setting the woods on fire. And man, I pulled that limo
over and walked right up to that son of a bitch and put
nine bullets of USA lead into his body, and I still wasn't
satisfied, but Jesus Christ you can hear the laws now,
and they're coming up, and so there's me and my gal,
and I'm yelling at her to get in the car, but I can't get
the bastard out of the seat—his body gone all squishy
and he is trapped behind the wheel and he is slippery
so's I can't get a purchase on him—and I hear them
coming and grab for the gun and turn, but it ain't no
law, it's a civ, but it seems like now I know him, like I
seen him before, and I guess I hesitated just a little too
long cuz 'fore I know it he's going for the gun and we're
struggling—but you know what's funny? it weren't really like we were fighting at all, more like some weird
dance, and I ain't no faggot, you understand, but I felt
better in that moment than I had ever felt before. I
was beautiful and graceful in the dance with my weird
man, and I wanted to hold onto him all night—until maybe he told me my real name—until maybe he
told me the name of my real father—until maybe—but

there weren't no maybe cuz later the boys told me there weren't nobody there, just me whirling and whirling, and besides while we were getting down to it, the laws really did come for real, and I hear my gal, my gal—my gal—I hear her say as she's jumping into the cop car, "He killed a man." And I think, "I sure done a lot more than that, little missy, I surely did."

And so I jumped back into the limo and sped away, and I knew I wasn't gonna make it but just wanted to give them a little chase is all, and when they finally got me, I had already figured out what I would say to the reporters when they came to ask me if I was sorry. I would say—this is what I would say—"At least for a little while, me and my gal—we had us some fun."

And then I'd go down like a hardass.

I think there is something not good in our America, baby. I think maybe we stirred it up by reaching so high. You know, you go looking for the New Jerusalem, and you're going to stir up the beast—lie with Leviathan in the deep deep.

And I think it's in me, too.

Anyway. I'm drunk.

But you know what? And after having said all that. The funny thing is that tomorrow morning, after this drunken tirade—O bad case of the demons, baby! Bad case!—I'm going to get up just like any other morning. And I'm going to brush my teeth and tie my shoes. And you know, it's funny, but life just goes on. I know that.

I understand that. And maybe, if you say that none of that stuff matters—O my lost fathers—and maybe, if in your eyes I can truly see that strange and wondrous truth that, you know, life really does just go on. O my baby. It's just license to shut the fuck up.

Silence.

Let the dead bury the dead.

Yeah.

So what do you say? Fuck the devil. Play that crazy horn, baby. And maybe maybe—walls come tumblin' down—and maybe baby—the walls of Jericho come silently tumbling down. Yeah. Go, cat, go!

A son is only half a man until he is an orphan of the heart.

[Click]......

Florida Gothic

Well, they took her away, you know. And she was shivering and sobbing all night in the jail cell. And she was yelling, "I'm so sorry!" And, "I never meant to."

And nobody had anything to say. There just ain't anything to say after something like that. She sure was pretty, though. Even after she had done what she had done. Sure was pretty.

As for him. He was two people, really. He was Pastor Bill, shepherd of the Gilead Assembly of God Church. And he was the scared man. The man who, push come to shove, couldn't make himself believe that he belonged anywhere but on the county backhoe he'd worked before the church called him. And he was scared his flock would realize it.

Yessir. There was two of him, all right. And this other Bill, the one who sometimes couldn't sleep Saturday nights worrying about the sermon and the deacon who didn't like him, still remembered his mama's tongue. That woman's words could sting. There's something about that mixed up in this mess, too.

Anyways. They all pretended to be shocked. But they weren't. It was to be expected. Liza was just trash. Weren't a man in the county, let alone the congregation, she hadn't flipped her hair at, crossing and uncrossing those legs like she was wet just looking at you. She was trouble. And Pastor Bill knew it, all right.

Well, I don't know what you'd want to say about

that. He had such a pretty wife at home.

Course they'd bought a new house. And the wife couldn't get pregnant. And it didn't seem to bother Bill much. But it sure did bother her.

And I expect it pleased the ladies in the church. All those mothers. You gotta throw that into the deal, too. It's only fair. Sure, they "oh my!"-ed and "bless her heart!"-ed. But they were happy that she didn't have any kids. Ladies like that? If they'd only known it, they would of liked to scratch her eyes out and snatch her head bald. Putting on airs like that. Who did she think she was, anyway? Miss America?

Course to her face they smiled real pretty.

She just didn't have no one to talk to.

"Bill, is that you?"

"Go back to sleep, hon."

"Where you been?"

"Had a meeting at the church."

"It's 12:30, Bill."

Seemed like she waited a long time. For him to say something.

"Well, it got over late. And some people wanted to talk," he said after awhile.

And the air conditioner was dripping.

And after awhile.

"I'm tired. Gonna take a shower."

And there was the bills too. Seems they were behind on the mortgage. And the credit cards were topped off. Bill bought her everything she wanted. And a whole

58

lot of stuff she didn't. Like they had it to spend. Like spending made it true.

And the church always needed something, too. The cinderblock building was only about ten years old, but they'd built it themselves. The congregation. Bill collectors calling about the truck. And she feared poverty.

Didn't take long until everybody knew about Liza and Pastor Bill. You couldn't help but notice. And what could you expect? Liza flaunted it, really. Hooked herself a Reverend. Man of God. Just like out of "The Thorn Birds". But nobody said anything to him for awhile. And I don't know what you'd want to say about something like that.

Pastor Bill wasn't talking. That's for sure. He was always tired. Tired like a man just all swallowed in horror. And getting up each morning and tying his tie. Like everything depended on his getting that tie knot just right. Things were moving fast.

"What are you doing?"

It was about three in the morning.

"I said what are you doing?"

But she was just standing there with the weed whacker.

"Answer me, dammit." His fists were clenched.

But she was just standing there in the moonlight. His wife. And she didn't have nothing on. In the front yard. Front yard of the house everybody knew belonged to Pastor Bill. With the weed whacker. Naked as the day she was born. Whack. Whack. Whack. His wife.

"God forgive me...."

He actually said that.

"God forgive me... sometimes I hate you," he said.

"Fuck you, Bill," she said. Very, very slowly. And loudly enough to make some dogs bark. She was smiling.

Course something had to be done. And hell, even Pastor Bill must of known that. Probably just what he wanted, don't you know. The Assemblies of God. They ain't just Holy Rollers no more. And ain't it just something to become respectable in America? Lot's of good folks done suffered a long time. Been snubbed. And ain't about to stand for it no more. Times are changing in America, you know.

And maybe Pastor Bill knew that better than most. And maybe he not only wanted to be caught, but maybe he wanted judgment. He'd been two people his whole life. Sooner or later a man gonna fall in love with what he fears. Sooner or later he's gonna wanna twist. Twist and burn bright like a bird in the flame.

"I need you."

She was just sitting there trembling.

"I'm talking to you. Say something."

She didn't.

"Dammit, honey, I love you."

She just kept on sitting.

"As your husband, I command you...."

But he couldn't even finish.

And then he started begging again. And crying. Big

snotty tears. Blubbering.

She was just trembling. And looking around. Like if she said something or looked him in the eye, she'd lose her rage. And sir, that was all she had.

It was all gone. They were gonna take the church away. You better believe it. He was gonna give a public apology tomorrow at the 10:30 service, ask for forgiveness and resign. And they couldn't keep the house. On account of how far behind they were. And the truck was all but repo-ed. It was over, sir.

"Jesus Christ! I've sinned, all right? Jesus forgives me. Why can't you?"

She was asleep on the couch. Anyways, she wanted him to think that. She wasn't sleeping. But he was standing over her half threatening-like in his briefs. She was on the couch in the living room. He'd been lying real conspicuous on the floor. On the floor next to the bed in the bedroom. In his briefs.

"Honey? You asleep?"

She could feel the vein in her forehead. It was just thumping.

"This is all your fault!" he was screaming.

It was about forty-five minutes later.

"This never would have happened if you were a real woman!" he said. Desperate-like.

And that vein was still thumping.

"You're wicked! You slut! You cunt! Get behind me Satan!"

He was making a cross with his fingers and putting it in her face. He was actually doing that.

"I'll do anything baby! Anything, please!"
Must have been about two by now. He was on his knees before her on the couch. In his briefs. He'd been smashing himself in the face as hard as he could. There wasn't any blood, but his temples looked bruised.
"If you'll just give me another chance..."
Thump. Thump.

About four he was finally asleep. And, by now, on the bed. Curled up in a fetal position. His left fist balled up and shoved in his eye. She was standing over him as he slept. And she sure was pretty.

Well, you saw it on the evening news as well as I did. The Pastor's wife stabbed him in the groin thirty-seven times. But, believe it or not, technically speaking, that's not what killed him. He was still living. She'd severed some artery. It was every step he took. Pumped the blood out of him. He was walking, and he was pumping blood out. With every step.

When they found him, he was on his knees and slumped over. Like a balloon three days after the party. He was gone, sir. And the blood was everywhere. He sat on his knees, and his head came to rest on the floor. His head supported him. It made his butt stick up a little. And the blood just dripped out of his briefs.

It was her who called 911. And she was there when they came.

"He was sleeping," she said.
She was just real calm, then.

And all this happened in Florida. And I saw it. I saw it all, sir. On the evening news.

And whatever else you'd want to say, she sure was pretty.

Trees (Illinois Noir)

The large-scale conversion of forests to croplands in the midwestern United States over the last century has led to a measurable cooling of the region's climate, according to NCAR scientist Gordon Bonan. The study, which appeared in the June issue of the Journal of Climate, is the first to document the link between regional climate change and a major change in temperate forest cover.

Human uses of land, especially clearing of forest for agriculture and reforestation of abandoned farmland, are an important cause of regional climate change," concludes Bonan. The cooling is the result of the changeover of the region to crops, which reflect more sunlight back into space than forests.

"Forest-to-cropland shift affects Midwestern temperatures"
(http://www.ucar.edu/communications/quarterly/summer01/forest.html0)

My people hated trees. Wasn't a tree in sight they didn't see as proof of evil ole Robin Goodfellow. Mr. Satan. Dark continence. Dark indifference.

Meat not souls.

They cleared the land. They cleared it all. They

ripped stumps from bleeding loamy loam and made the land geometric. Uh-huh. They grew the crops they wanted. They lived and prospered.

The American farmer.

I suppose it amounts to what you owe. What they can pin on you. Everybody has a price. A moral price. What they'll own to when it all comes down. When it all comes down and it's clear that something is going to have to be paid. When the shit came down, I copped to plenty.

•

The only thing about her that could be true was that nothing about her could be true. Linda Lorning Steadman was not your ordinary girl.

When she walked into my office I immediately recognized the situation. I did not resist. I stood up and walked around the desk. She raised her cigarette to her lips. Thumbnail flick. I am holding the match. There is lipstick.

"Yes," she said, touching my hand to steady the flame, "you'll do."

She blew out the match.

I blew the smoke back in her face.

She smiled. "A man with pride?" Her eyebrows arched.

"Keep peddling it, lady. I'm buying."

After the Gulf War I ended up in Kankakee. I took a job with the K-Mart Distribution Center. Then with the School District. There was a wife and a house. I wasn't any good at it. I started selling real estate about the time Bourbonnais exploded. They took the prairie and the farms. Cleared it all. Anybody with any money left Kankakee. Yeah. They just left. Moved next door. They built subdivisions. They built five bedroom-and-three-car garages in Bourbonnais and listened to Celine Dion on built-in home entertainment systems. Planted trees as windbreaks. Next door.

I couldn't get a job in Bourbonnais. Stayed in Kankakee carrying listings nobody wanted: Once-desirable river front property. Mom and Pop cottages on quiet streets behind the tracks. Shabby farm-and-railroad-money mansions with weeds in the concrete cracks of driveways. Uh-huh. Listening to something else.

Her husband, Steve, was a Trust Fund Baby. Eldest and only of the scion of Kankakee. He was a Steadman. Wealthiest family in town. Owned a full third of the commercial real estate. The family. Powerful family. He'd met Linda in Vegas in the midst of a messy divorce. She was where she needed to be. He was your usual cocained-and-wreck-the-expensive-car kind of kid. But he wasn't a kid anymore. And time was running out.

Franklin Steadman—Frank—the father, riddled with prostate cancer, was an inordinately proud man and an indulgent parent. Couldn't say "no". Co-signed loans. Steve had been the first and only. They'd tried so hard to have a son. Finally had to adopt. Steve had made promissory notes to his adoptive dad to pay back losses from deals gone bad. And there were a lot of deals gone bad.

Betty, the second wife, former mistress, was the problem. She'd replaced the first wife when Steve was fifteen. Now, a bitter, used-up woman, she spent her time drinking vodka gimlets and fantasizing revenge. She, herself, had been replaced in Frank's arms, many times over. She had stopped traffic in her day. She would surely press the notes.

Two weeks later. Linda pulled the sheet over her breasts. "So that's the lay," she said. "The promissory notes. The old man can't last in his condition. He's finished. The Fed took it all in the Savings and Loan deal. If he dies, there won't be anything left. And we'll... I'll... you and me... will end up paying. I've got plenty stashed away, but Steve is weak. If they find those notes we'll be on the tip. You've got to get them."

I saw the logic.

•

Betty Steadman was not unattractive. At fifty-three (her husband, Frank, was a cool seventy-six), she was handsome. But she had been beautiful. Former home wrecker. I figured I could make her remember.

I had some contacts through some colleagues. Got word around that I might have a buyer for the Steadman mansion. Decaying tennis courts. Cracked fountains. Weeds in the garden. There was no buyer.

Betty came to the door boozy and breasty.

"Won't you take a seat?"

I chose a stark leather affair. Scandinavian, circa 1973.

"Care for a drink?"

"I never drink before noon."

"I never trust a man who doesn't drink before noon."

"I would hate for you to mistrust me."

"Scotch?"

"Make it neat."

When she came back with the drink I could smell her hair. She leaned over to make sure I got an eyeful.

I did.

She gave me a key when I left several hours later. "You can show the house anytime you want." She dismissed me with a kiss. I had been a good boy. For several hours.

Outside, the trees, thick down by the river, did not move in the humidity. I knew how they felt. I wanted a shower. I got in my machine. Parked in the driveway. Next time I would park on the street. Around the corner. It was arranged. I could still taste her. She had been a wild woman. She had begged me to hit her. I did. She had wept against my chest. I held her. She had clawed my back. It stung. Her sad, sagging, infirm breasts. I had made her remember.

I drove to the office.

●

The phone rang. It would be Linda.

"I'm in," I said.

"The promissory notes are in the office. In the desk. In a manilla folder. Get the manilla folder."

"I'm going back on Wednesday. Frank's in Chicago."

"I love you," she said.

"Can I see you tonight?"

"Be patient. I think Steve is getting suspicious."

"I want you."

"Be a good boy."

I was.

●

It was late. I'd been sleeping. The sound was the phone.

"You've got to come! Right now!"

"Linda? Where are you?"

"O God! Something terrible has happened."

"Where are you?"

"Please..."

"Linda, it will be alright. Just tell me where you are."

"I'm at the Steadman's."

I was there in ten minutes.

The house was dark. Linda was sobbing quietly in the living room. The bedroom door was open. Betty lay by the bed, her face beaten in. Beside her was a bloodied bronze paperweight. It was a replica of the John Hancock Building.

"It was Steve! O God! He was crazy! I've never seen him like that. He was so coked up… I tried to stop him."

I buried her face in my chest. She trembled. She sobbed.

"It's OK, it's OK…" I whispered.

"I tried to stop him. I followed him here. I pleaded with him. You have to believe me, I never meant for this to happen."

"Shush, baby, of course not." But something was not right.

"Somehow he'd found out about you and her…"

I froze.

"About me and her?"

She said nothing.

"How did he find out about Betty and me?"

She paused.

"Oh darling, please forgive me…" She burst into sobs.

"You told him?"

"Yes, don't you see? I had to."

I didn't see.

"It's perfect. No one would ever convict you. He's a known cocaine addict."

"What?"

"Don't be so stupid. He comes for you in a jealous rage and…"

"You mean you meant for me to kill him?"

"In self-defense."

I paused. I was beginning to sense the logic.

"But why Betty? Why would he be so crazy jealous over her...?"

"You don't think she stayed at home all day and played Solitaire do you?"

Betty and Steve. I saw some more logic.

"It's been going on for months."

"And this was common knowledge?"

"As common as her," she spit out. She buried her face in her hands, sobbing suddenly. "I'm sorry, that was such an ugly thing to say... especially now."

Yes. Now. Betty's bashed in face still lay beside the bed.

"We've got to get out of here."

"No! First get the notes!"

I went into the office. Opened the drawer. The manila folder was where she said it would be. The manila folder. It seemed light.

"Quickly!" She pressed something into my hand. It was a gun. It would be registered to Steven Steadman. It would go off in a struggle. He'd be out of the way. Linda and me. We thought alike. She was just a whole lot quicker.

I smiled at her.

She smiled back.

"Just how much do you have stashed away?"

"Later, darling. We've got to find Steve."

"Yes. Steve."

•

We went to the office. She called. We sat in the dark. We waited. We waited some more. And then he came.

He seemed quite cool actually. Not like a man who had just beaten his step-mother lover to death with a bronze paperweight. And Linda. She didn't seem that frightened. I began to wonder. Sometimes you think you understand the con. Sometimes you're wrong.

"What's this all about Linda? I got your message," he said.

"Hello darling." He lit the cigarette she had put to her lips. "How's Betty?"

I played it cool. Waiting.

"Betty?"

"Yes, mama dearest."

"Linda... I don't understand..."

"Don't you? Surely the old man told you."

"Told me what? You're talking crazy. And who is this?"

"Just a friend, pal," I said.

He looked confused. Weary.

"So he never told you? I see. Well, he wouldn't, would he? Never mind, there will be time enough for everything."

"Linda, enough of this. I'm not playing your games anymore." He said it as if he'd said it a thousand times. As if it were just something he said anymore.

"Well, let's just see. Shall we take a ride?"

He didn't have anything. He had sold what mattered a long time ago.

We walked to my machine parked out front.

"Linda, what's this all about?" I whispered as Steve got in the back seat.

"It's nothing darling, everything's under control."

"But..."

"Shhh..." She touched my lips. "I need a witness."

A witness. I had already bought the ticket.

In the car she turned around and handed Steve a slip of white paper.

"I brought you a present."

He didn't say anything. He rolled a bill and the powder was gone.

"Feel better?"

He didn't say anything.

"Where to?" I whispered.

"The Steadman's."

I pulled out into the Kankakee night.

•

It was a quiet ride. Through beat streets. Kids shot BB guns at streetlights. I did not think. Did not resist. You buy the ticket. You take the ride. Old Mexicans with ancient eyes sat in chairs on the sidewalk and watched the flashing yellow traffic lights. It was late. They didn't care where we were going. I took the ride.

When we got to the house, Steve was high. Alert.

"Come here, honey," she said without turning on the lights, "I want you to see something."

He followed.

I stayed in the living room. I saw the light go on in the bedroom. I heard the cry. I heard his howl. I heard her voice telling him something. Telling him something. He stopped howling. He'd heard something. He came from the room, his clothes all bloody. His eyes were wild and then suddenly dead.

It was as if the drug had gone to his hair. It was ridiculously spiked and smeared with blood. The moonlight played like blonde highlights on its tips. He was clutching the bloody John Hancock. Kneading it. He opened and closed his eyes. But he was already dead. Something had already killed him.

She came from the bedroom. She was smiling as if at a cocktail party. She led him to a chair and then I watched as she leaned close to him and whispered something in his ear. He tried to get up and then sat back down. He opened and closed his eyes. His dead eyes. She handed him the rubber tube. He tied it on his arm. She handed him the needle. He placed it on the vein. She nodded. He pushed the plunger and shuddered. He began to turn blue surprisingly quick. He was already gone.

"That's a good boy," she said.

•

We waited. And then we waited some more. By the time it was time to stop waiting, I wasn't surprised at all to see the old man. He didn't seem all that surprised to see us either. She'd called him. Of course. Arranged it.

"Hello Frank."

"Linda? It's dark in here. Who's that with you?"

"Oh don't mind him, Frank. He's a friend."

"Who's that?" He pointed to the still figure in the chair.

"Shall we turn on the light and see?"

She turned on the light.

He clutched at his chest.

"Stevie!"

"It's your son, Papa." Her words were like slaps across his frail face. It's my husband, Papa." He seemed to be reeling. "It's my brother, Papa."

The old man stared at his son. His hands. Paper-thin. They fluttered helplessly.

"I guess he couldn't stand it anymore. He seems to have given himself an overdose. I wonder what it was that he couldn't stand? Did you know that he was fucking Betty?"

The old man looked up. His face twitched. Sunken. He reached for a chair. He sat down.

"He needed an older woman to replace his mother. You remember her, don't you? Your first wife. Stella. You were married twenty years. Surely you remember her, Papa? The one who couldn't give you a son, let alone a daughter. The one who stayed at home while you fucked your ever-fertile whore in Vegas. What was the whore's name now? Let me see. B. Starts with a B..."

"Betty! No!" He sprang up as if the chair were

electric. His paper-thin hands. He looked to the bedroom.

"That's right, old man. Her name was Betty. Mother of two. Although I don't remember the girl. Didn't Betty give her up for adoption? That's right. Now what were their names? The "adoptive parents"? Lorning. Yes, that's it. Your nanny and her husband. And you, old man, you didn't see her either, did you? Not until she was sixteen anyway. Sixteen. Isn't that a lovely age, old man? Aren't those little sixteen year-old girls just irresistible, old man? Set her up in Vegas, if I remember. Made her your new mistress. Just like her mama."

Very slowly, the old man began walking to the bedroom. He walked because it was there to be done. Because it was unavoidable.

He entered the bedroom.

"Oh did I forget to tell you old man?" she called after him. "Seems little Stevie killed his mother before he offed himself. Seems as if he just went crazy."

The old man came to the door.

She pulled out the manila folder. The manila folder.

She threw it at his feet. The folder opened up. Two official looking documents slid out before him. Two birth certificates. Linda Marie Steadman. Steven Alan Steadman.

"You bastard. They were there all the time. Didn't even bother to lock them up. Didn't even bother to hide them."

"I..."

"Never thought anyone would find them? Originals

after you paid the county boys to accept your doctored copies. Imagine my surprise. Yes, I was looking for little Stevie's promissory notes. And all the while these birth certificates were sitting in your desk. Unlocked."

The old man stood in the doorway.

She turned to me. "Give me the gun."

"What are you going to do?"

"Give it to me!"

I reached into my pocket and took it out.

"Here's what you're going to do Papa. You are going to destroy those birth certificates. And then you are going to postdate and sign this statement for the police." She pulled out two pages of neatly typed script. "It says that you came home unexpectedly to find that your son had murdered your wife and daughter-in-law in a drug induced frenzy. And then you are going to shoot me with that gun."

He opened his mouth.

"Shut up, old man. You're going to shoot me until I'm dead and then you are going to live—for as long as you do live—knowing that you killed your own daughter. You are going to do it because you are proud."

He lifted his hand. And then let it fall.

"You are going to do it because I can hurt you more dead than alive now. Look at me old man! You will live knowing that your son killed your wife and his mother because of you. But you will tell no one. And you will know that your son killed himself because he found out who you really are. Your only son, old man. Heir to nothing. And you will tell no one. And it will kill you. Not the cancer, old man. But the truth. And you will live with that secret until you die. And you will tell no one. And you will die alone."

"I...."

"You will do it—or this man will tell the world what really happened."

They both looked at me. The witness.

"Don't worry," she said to me, "you'll be paid. Everything I've stashed away—it's two and a half million..." The old man flashed a look at her. "Yes, two and a half million—little Stevie has been bilking you for years. There is two and a half million in an off-shore account—and I've signed it over to you."

"But..." I started.

"Don't bother," she said, "you'll take it."

I opened my mouth again. The witness.

"You'll take it. You recognize the situation. You and I, we think alike."

I said nothing.

"Now give me the gun."

I looked at her.

And then I shot the old man.

•

My people would have been proud. My people who ripped stumps from bleeding loamy loam and felt virtuous. As for me—no longer virtuous—no longer with the possibility of virtue—I copped to plenty. It was my turn. Yeah. And sometimes. Sometimes we all get what we deserve.

I took the rap for the old man. Linda took the rest.

There's a moratorium on the death penalty in the state of Illinois. I expect she will live a very long time. And so will I. Witnessing.

Illinois Forests
Illinois was surveyed by the United States General Land Office between 1807 and 1844. Notes kept by surveyors provide a glimpse at the early Illinois landscape. About 38% of the state (13.8 million acres) was forested, 61% was prairie, and less than 1% was water. Settlement changed the face of the landscape quickly as prairies were converted to cropland and trees were cut for fuel, building materials, and commercial sale.
(http://www.inhs.uiuc.edu/dnr/fur/habitats/ilinfrst.html)

Beyond the Piney Wood

How could we sing the LORD's song in a foreign land?
If I forget you, O Jerusalem, let my right hand wither!
Let my tongue cling to the roof of my mouth, if I do
not remember you, if I do not set Jerusalem above my
highest joy.
—Psalm 137: 4-6

Well, I don't know what you'd expect, but I'd killed
a man in a piney wood at just about dusk—and the sky
the color of blue porcelain pitchers of milk, and the
wind-whipped frost flying up the cuff of my coat, and it
snowing white in the yellow moon—and how what I'd
remembered most after the sound and scent of the shot
was the sound of soft and then brittle needles beneath
my boots and the smell of the trees and the blood and
his horse, and wood smoke—and so you put that all together, and I guess I'd turned my back on something or
another, like kindly finally forgetting to sit facing the
door when stakes are high and me holding dead man's
hand just like Wild Bill in Deadwood (I do not care for
your parlors, pillars, and strawberry socials, your col-
umns, quadrilles, and Daughters of the Confederacy),
and so I lit out and did not look back—raise the black
flag!—turned my face against one and all.

Can't say as anybody did miss me—I did not, no,
did not hear no bitter cries of remorse nor sorrow
when spurs hit terrified stolen horse all a sudden-like

and flecks from her foam hit my face and I dashed into darkness beyond the piney wood—ain't got no wife nor kid, and me mother never shed no tear, no, not one snuffle from first day hence, least-a-ways not on my account.

Don't even know if she's still living.

This lady, my Mama—nothing but a small-poxed whore who would not hesitate to go with anyone if there were greenback and liquor involved, even Injuns who come stinking of Government bonded and tobacco and old blankets—and Daddy, well he never had no name himself as near as I can tell—poor boy blown out from some Buckeye farm to places where we had better not talk about in just this light from the campfire, my friends, and so let's just say he "gone to Texas" (or just "GTT" like the old signs use to say on doors back east where there'd been a bit of trouble and some cussed mother's son gone down that outlaw trail)—and I never knew him, just one more blind fuck on a corn cob mattress—and ain't no love-loss between Mama and me, neither.

And so as I'd lived just about everywhere in these United States—these stars of my republic now hanging brutal and pious over plantation grounds across which my people never sauntered, nor to which even invited once to luncheon, and yet for which I flung my poor Confederate carcass down in seas of mud and blood and useless dying because I happened to be in Missouri and not Kansas when the raiders came and signed me up—

(Got to laugh at these contingencies, my fellow

watchmen of the night—you who drive the cattle and sometimes do not return home…)

—And so as I've lived just about everywhere. Followed troops with Mama in one or other scattered minor Indian skirmish when just a pup, even once down into Texas, 'cause with soldiers there's gotta be some action and a woman's gotta eat, and I, myself at tender years, used to pimp her in trading posts which nobody could remember ever having set up and last chance mining camps and once even at a soul-spavined Dakota farm everybody'd thought abandoned, until word got out that the father'd only gone crazy and shot the mother and kids and was crazy lonesome out there for gooseberry preserves from Massachusetts and maybe a need to procreate to replace what he'd taken—or just struck with sorrow of this horniness all alone out there on the impassive prairie—and so trekked out there, me and Mama, across unspeakable wastes, and went begging on off chance of some money and maybe a marriage, and did not get shot nor killed but survived to move on, always moving on, even now, out here on this range so big you'd think there must be no end to moving on, just gradual refinement of movement until it ain't no different from lying down out here in such meadow grass and becoming something the land recognizes and accepts as her own.

And so, like I've been saying, since I have never known home, this lighting out after my assignation in the piney woods, gunpowder in my nose and moon in my eyes, after this it was no big thing for me to move on, move on, and I lit out and did not look back—raise the black flag!—turned my face against one and all.

I was there, you know, when Quantrill took Lawrence, Kansas, and 142 mother's sons died, and the
town gutted and thick with greasy flames and woman-
ish shrieks and grown abolitionists hiding 'neath the
wooden seats of stinking privies in fear and wild-eyed
exaltation, and Cole Younger and Frank James rode
with us.

We rode in at dawn after a more than two-day
march, and some of the boys strapped to their horses
to keep from falling off 'cause we'd been on the road for
so long and never stopping here nor there and sleeping
in caves, and we were wearing our red flannels and hats
pulled down o'er eyes, and we were full of bile-throated
need for vengeance—'cause you know of the outrag-
es and the perfidy of those Red Legs and Jayhawkers,
dontcha? not least of whom was that no account savage
Jim Lane who later got ole General Thomas Ewing to
issue damnable Order No. 11 which dispossessed families from land and kin and cut off kids from homes
all across Jackson, Cass, Bates, and even parts of Ver-
non counties in Missouri, and him, Jim Lane, that Red
Leg traitor to no less than manhood did not spare the
women nor children in his own raids but slaughtered
and raped and pillaged with impunity the occupied
towns across the border and so was number one man
on Quantrill's list to capture and bring back to Missouri for public hanging in Jackson County.

And that wasn't all neither, 'cause I don't know what

you know, but they got our women—all women who may or may not have been lovers, wives, or sisters of Quantrill's boys—and put 'em in a brick building under arrest until the Kansas wind come and blew down the crumbly old building and killed our fair maidens from our hearths and our beds and our hearts, and even Bloody Bill Anderson lost his two sisters, and because it was in Lawrence that this had happened, and because it was in Lawrence that they kept the booty stolen from Missouri farms, and because it was in Lawrence that we could see the shape so clearly of such boiling hate and humiliation (and boys, think on all the things in this damned life that just never shoulda happened), and because it was Lawrence, we set upon them at dawn like an army of locusts in our red flannels, and in places the melee got out of hand and liquor stores were broken into and fueled the fighting, and shots were fired madly into burning buildings, and I can say at least this: not one woman was murdered, raped, nor handled unchivalrously—nor child neither—but I saw an old man cut with a carving knife before the eyes of his own family until he slowly bled to death and his stomach lay steaming in the dust, and the blank expression on his woman's face was just like how the clouds hanging over this land don't reveal nothing 'bout what they truly think about what's going on here below, and I myself shot and took my pleasure in the killing—and was a warrior, and a hero—and though they would not give our Quantrill a commission, I was a patriot in the Glorious Cause.

But no, my fellow range rovers of the cattle drive

night, this was not exactly how it was at all.

There was no Glorious Cause, and I had no fight nor feud with the people of Kansas, nor Union nor Confederate cause. The raiders approached me when I lay huddled in a barn hiding out from all and sundry 'cause I'd killed a man in a piney wood—just looking for a place to sleep—and they said to me, are you a damned Jayhawker or Red Leg? and me I says back, no sir, I'm nothing, and they said, well, what you doing in this place at this time? and I said, I'm just here is all, and they made like to kill me right then because I could have been a spy, and so I told them that the bluecoats got my brother and I went out looking for an eye for an eye and please don't tell no one because my Mama would surely skin me alive for lighting out like that, and then they laughed and took me with them and gave me a horse and a gun—and after awhile it just gets to be your life.

And so I do not know if I was a warrior and a hero, but for a while anyway I was, 'cause that's what we all were, and there were a whole lot of people back then that wanted to shake my hand.

And oh, yes, I drifted and joined up here and there, and then when it was all over, rode the rails, was one of them hoboes—hoe boys—one of those proud veterans you all's Mamas honored in your town squares, if they still had them, or ever had—was one of the boys who'd taken their tools of the Cain-trade to find work, upon coming home and finding all lost and destroyed and burnt, with no compassion nor tears, just business proposition, you understand—and with malice toward none.

And so, yes, I took off then, too, and sometimes had to ride a-top them old boxcars 'cause no room in the inn—no room for one more laborer on the inside—and the coal smoke black and thick on my face until all us coal-Cain sumbitches laughed at one another, and it was just like being in one genuine Stephen Foster of a minstrel show, and sang "Hard Times" and "O Susanna" and "Camptown Ladies Sing this Song"—doo dah, doo dah—and we were laughing 'cause it was really truly something to be set free like this again, unmoored and unbounded—it was like the war all over again—and the free-fall never stopped, and it was not all that different from crying with great big gasps and chokes and snot running down your face, and I saw many a man step to the door to get his fair share of fresh air, and another man push him out into great open nothing of this our republic for the sheer meanness of it.

And from my moving throne, I saw things you can't begin to imagine nor tell, because such destruction and devastation does not have a name and in the end is about the taking away of names anyway, until there's nothing left but just brutal sounds and gestures, and it tears a man up inside to have to wordlessly claw at such spectacles as these with neither sentences nor paragraphs nor inclination to hide his face no more—they took the eyelids off this nation, boys, and you can't never shut your eyes again.

I saw belles in bustles filling their blushed cheeks

with clods of dirt. I saw broken fiddles and men dancing without a beat. I saw hunger walking on two legs like a man, and churches where the pews were still bloody, and old style Presbyterian Puritan Pastors weeping into hands that no longer remembered how bravely they had once waved and pounded the pulpit, and nowhere did I find work or sustenance that I did not steal from families and farms that already could not support their dazed occupants—and yes, I lit out then as well, and kept moving in this reconstructed southern Union and could not find a place to stop where I did not see the skeleton of a chimney of some burnt out home in some naked, bald, dark hollow.

Drifted on.

And oh, my boys, do not stop me now—I am singing, I am singing—and do not, no don't give me no more shit about burying me in my boots in my dying time, 'cause I don't want to lie out here so lonesome and drear. No, boys, take me home when I go. Bring me back to some place where I can rest, or I swear I will haunt you forever, until you see me always a-walking, always a-coming, and never arriving, and you waiting, always and forever, for something that never comes. I will haunt you, because that's what haunting is: never letting go of what is never there.

You think that's funny? The next one of you fucks who so much as cracks a smile at me, I will kill.

Oh, I'm a fucked up drunk now—don't you think I know that?—but I tell you, me and the boys, we had us some fun. Been shot fourteen times, and got the stiffness on cold mornings to prove it. Still, wouldn't know it to look at me now, but I was a fine buck in me day. Oh, and the refinement! That was part of it, too. We were well-dressed and well-groomed. Trimmed our beards even to hit a train. Beyond the piney woods lie whole continents of glamour. We were brave and daring—once even read in a newspaper how a man at one of the banks said that we were courteous, and it was an honor to be robbed by men such as we. Makes me proud, even now. Fruit of the Union.

Turned my back against one and all—raise the black flag!—but, gotta admit, did not anticipate the adulation, the praise, the longing to be what I was without the consequences. This country surely loves a killer.

I can see that you don't believe me. Just one more old fuck going on. That's alright. We tell the tall tale out here in the West. It's true enough, though, and I don't give a damn about who knows it. I rode with the best of 'em. Even Jesse and Frank once, though I'm not exactly at liberty to talk about that (Frank is still living, you know, and Cole and Jim Younger gonna be free men someday).

No I don't care… who knows it.

Always got a place to stay if I need it in Missouri, Arkansas, Kansas City.

I'm petering out boys. It's late, and sun'll be here before we know it. Pass that bottle.

We got a long way to go 'fore the drive is done.

I didn't mean nothing earlier.
Wouldn't a kilt nobody. Gun wasn't even loaded.
I'm just feeling a little ornery, that's all.
Feeling a little dark.
Pass that bottle, would ya?

Ah Mama. I'm dreaming now, and it is always to you I return in my dreams. I'm dreaming, and so the words just keep coming—don't dream proper no more, just keep talking to myself, never slip off into other voices cause I just can't afford to let down my guard even now. Always on the run, Mama. Been on the run for too long, now.

You know how when you wake up and the sun ain't there yet, and you know that you got an hour or so to sleep, and you want to slip back down but just can't, so you continue on somewhere in-between being who you are when other people are around and who you are in dreams? Well, that's what it's like now. I'm dreaming, Mama, and I always know I'm dreaming. The words just don't stop. And it's always my own voice. Been so long now since I've dreamt and not known it. Always dreaming and always watching my back, and never waking up no more, Mama.

Twilighting, really. That's what it is, twilighting—life just not making up its mind to be one thing or another, nighttime or day, poem or prose, fiction or time of no shadows at noon with gun in your hand and not no time, no not no time at all, to think.

Ah, Mama. Coming back to you in my dreams that

aren't even proper dreams.

You were not pretty nor good nor kind, but all that I had, and you fed me, too. Pox come and took your face away, but that was before I was let in and the door opened and me popped out of you all bloody and squalling, and I don't really know what proto-pox first set you a-reeling adrift in this land, because there must of been something else, something that come before what came. I expect your people were Irish, and I've never known a Murphy to stay at home. And Daddy, well, who knows? You told me of that night and how you knew you was gonna get pregnant but went ahead anyway and didn't even do all those deep mysteries you did to keep from finding fruit from your nightly labors, like Penelope in that book you gave me when we were near out of bread and cheese but still stupidly full of hope for a home—like Penelope unravelling her day each night against the raids on the past, against the inevitability of her one true husband never coming home over hill—until finally, unlike Penelope, you must of just give up, and if not Odysseus then Telemachus, and so you let me in, let me into this world, opened the door and out I come, and so I guess I had to love you, though I don't think this is what folks mean proper when they talk of love. It was just following. You, my forever promisedland, and me, blindly dashing behind you into dark night of your never being pretty but at least cheap, what with the pox and your face gone, and so this love seems really to be nothing more than a not being able to sit still, but I miss you now, truth be told. I miss seeing your back and me trotting behind. I miss there being someone to follow, Mama.

Ah yes, and now it's the riders coming in. Always the riders riding hard and fierce. They come in at night and sweep me on up until sometimes I'm among them and it is me shooting up the town and the folks hiding behind doors knowing enough to keep out of the rain, knowing enough to keep to themselves while we swoop on into the bank and flash cold steel and six-gun and stacks of greenback hefted up from drawers somewhere fairly steaming like sweet chunks of sod on a spade and whumped on into gunny sacks, and shots and more metal-smoke sulfur smell as we are off and out into the day of hard riding away, always just ahead of the posse and at least in the early days, happy and shouting 'cause we knowed they just didn't have it in them to chase us down and shoot us in holes like dogs when wounded tired and sleepy weary from always on the road with a gun at our back behind every tree—

Ah, the riders are coming in Mama, and other times they be bluecoats, or column behind column of Johnny Reb behind the Stars and Bars and somebody shouting out a tuneless Dixie, and there are drummer boys, too, sometimes—always the riders named police and cop and law and making sure you don't settle nowhere, riders of American apocalypse, which is simply principle of never settling down but forever moving on, moving on just like boxcars and Buffalo ghosts forever.

And the riders come and take me back, back always leading to you and your original turning back on it all, your own original dash beyond the piney wood, because you are no longer just Mama no more but the land herself, the nation—the New Jerusalem of my true citizenship. You are before and beyond and the door opening both into my own inevitable-like original sin moment in the piney wood and also back into endless days of creation when God himself took the great leap beyond the piney wood and set it all a-reeling, and Mama, ah Mama, the man I shot in the piney wood, I shot him in the back, and I weren't no more than fifteen, and he never did me no harm. I just shot him because it was there to be done, and that was my first act, my first deed, and it is in this original act, in this first deed, that the door is opened, and I learn to breathe in the piney wood, and I learn to walk like a man only when I make the dash myself.

Out into great, dark, starless night, Mama—beyond the piney wood.

Leon

We have come upon a very different age from any that preceded us... Yesterday, and ever since history began, men were related to one another as individuals... Today, the everyday relationships of men are largely with great impersonal concerns, with organizations, not with other individual men... Now this is nothing short of a new social age, a new era of human relationships, a new stage-setting for the drama of life.
—Woodrow Wilson, 1912

Friday, September 6, 1901. Turn of the century, Mr. Czolgosz, turn of the century. Telephone ringing. America calling. Blood dripping.

Hey, it's for you, Leon. Leon Czolgosz. Will you take it?

And a voice says, "Bang, bang, you're dead, Mr. McKinley." President William McKinley from Ohio, where they love him because he stands for all that is brave and right and white in America, and because, like somebody else would say later, "the business of America is business," and where they have just elected him for a second term, and we are morally perfectible, and it is the American century and the culmination of Carnegie and Frick and Rockefeller and Morgan and Vanderbilt and—Mr. President from Ohio!

And well, you know, orders are orders. What's a poor boy to do? Two shots in the stomach and they send you to the chair, Leon. Ha, ha. Laugh out loud. They barely even gave you a trial.

You fool. You cipher. You patsy.

Didn't your mama ever tell you? You can't kill Leviathan. You can't kill the Octopus. You can't kill Capital at the turn of the century at the Temple of Music at the Pan-American Exposition in Buffalo in 1901. No way. No how.

Oh Leon! Leon. You laid the president down. And you shot the president down. Just tell me this. Just tell me this one thing.

How does it feel to have a face, Mr. Czolgosz?

For the rest, at a time when the universality of Spirit has gathered such strength, and the singular detail, as is fitting, has become correspondingly less important, when, too, that universal aspect claims and holds on to the whole range of the wealth it has developed, the share in the total work of Spirit which falls to the individual can only be very small. Because of this, the individual must all the more forget himself, as the nature of Science implies and requires. Of course, he must make of himself and achieve what he can; but less must be demanded of him, just as he in turn can expect less of himself, and may demand less for himself.

—G.W.F. Hegel, 1807

Tick. Tick. Tick. Clock is ticking, Leon. You are crazy. And you know it. 1898. Cleveland. You work in the wire mill. You work 12 hours a day, six days a week, 52 weeks a year—because this is a Christian nation and you get the Sabbath off. The fucking Sabbath, Leon. And on the Sabbath you go to Socialist meetings. And you go to Anarchist meetings. And you learn that all rulers are the enemies of the people. It is a good thing to kill the enemies of the people, Leon. This is what you learn. You are crazy, and you know it.

Tick.

Tick. Tick.

I hear the keening of Cleveland in 1898. Nightmare chimneys. Horse hooves on cobble stones. There is a child. The stench! They make you live like a beast, Mr. Czolgosz. And when it snows the snow turns black.

What's her name? The woman you watch? I know that there is a woman that you watch. Her name is Maria, right? Must be Maria. You and all the other Poles— the women you watch—they are all named Maria. Mother of God. Stella Maris. Star of the sea. The star that guides all sailors home.

But you can't see no stars in the Cleveland night of 1898, Leon. You ain't no Copernicus. And besides, they sold them. That's right. Sold the fucking stars. Star of Bethlehem. And you saw them do it, too, man.

You watched her—the woman you watch—and you followed her into great white night until you saw the electric light burning in her window—red light burning in her window!—and the door opening and closing. And the men coming and going. And the men coming and going. And you stood out in the alley watching the men coming and going, Leon. And you know, it wasn't like something cracked in you or something. It was like something so quietly and inevitably rolled over. The sigh of your mother. Your dead mother. And she rolled over. And it just ain't never been the same Leon. Ain't never been the same.

So what did you do? Oh man! You fool, you goof, you holy idiot. You got quiet, Leon. You got real quiet. And the family just didn't understand. And in 1898 you walked into the factory mill, and with invisible weapons you slew the horrible beasts. Ancient dignity. You stood up straight. With swords that did not exist you pierced the foul breast of your foreman. You sallied forth. You danced. You whooped hollers. And then you collapsed and foamed at the mouth (no shit!)—you crazy mother-fucker—and they carried you out and forgot your stupid unpronounceable name, Leon Czolgosz, forgot your name. And truth be told they never had no use for your name to begin with. Cleveland, 1898. How stupid can you get? How is it that you got this far in life and never understood that you are invisible, faceless? You do not matter. You are nobody. Welcome to America, Leon. There are a thousand more where you came from. Fuck you.

The collective is a body, too. And the physis that is being organized for it in technology can, through all its political and factual reality, only be produced in that image sphere to which profane illumination initiates us. Only when in technology body and image so interpenetrate that all revolutionary tension becomes bodily collective innervation, and all the bodily innervations of the collective become revolutionary discharge, has reality transcended itself to the extent demanded by the Communist

Manifesto. For the moment, only the Surrealists have understood its present commands. They exchange, to a man, the play of human features for the face of an alarm clock that in each minute rings for sixty seconds.

—Walter Benjamin, 1929

Buffalo, New York. 1901. Pan-American Exposition. Ring, ring, ring. America calling. And hey! Ain't we grown up, yet? Alexander Graham Bell. Thomas Alva Edison. Hey! We're waiting for you, Mr. Ford, Mr. Bill Gates.

But nevermind that now. It's 1901. It's the Pan-American Exposition. First of the great fairs to commemorate no actual historical event at all whatsoever. Ha, ha, ha. Laugh out loud. And that's just fine. Because America is the event, itself. The ahistorical event. America. And the age of Electricity and Progress.

Check it out, man. Center of the exposition. It's the Electric Tower. We're talking 44,000 lights. We're talking power. We're talking the Spanish-American War. We're talking a searchlight at the top of the 325 foot tall American tower of Babel that can be seen from Canada and Niagara in 1901. Oh, man! We're talking the city on the hill (O my America!).

And the buildings of the exposition. Too funny. Rainiest season in years. And get this: the buildings are not meant to be permanent. ("And everyone who hears these words of mine and does not act on them will be like a foolish man who built his house on sand. The rain fell, and the floods came, and the winds blew and beat against that house, and it fell—and great was its fall!") Joke's on us. Plaster and chicken wire. And the rain. And even within weeks of the opening, the buildings are visibly falling apart. Drip, drip, drip. Laugh out loud. And the seams. And the seams. Oh Leon! America is falling apart.

Turn of the century.

Revenge, working men! To arms! Your masters sent out their bloodhounds—the police. They killed six of your brothers at McCormick's this afternoon. They killed the poor wretches, because they, like you, had the courage to disobey the supreme will of your bosses... You have for years endured the most abject humiliation; you have for years suffered immeasurable iniquities; you have worked yourselves to death; you have endured the pangs of want and hunger; your children you have sacrificed to the factory lords... Why? To satisfy the insatiable greed to fill the coffers of your lazy, thieving master. When you ask them now to lessen your burden he sends his bloodhounds out to shoot you, kill you. If you are men, if you are the sons of your grandsires who have shed their blood to free you, then you will rise in your might, Hercules, and destroy the hideous monster that seeks to destroy you. To arms we call you! To arms!

—"Revenge!" circular printed immediately after the Haymarket Massacre, Chicago, 1886

America is calling, Leon. America is calling.

Then, faint and prolonged, across the levels of the ranch, he heard the engine whistling for Bonneville... and abruptly Presley saw again, in his imagination, the galloping monster, the terror of steel and steam, with its single eye, cyclopean, red, shooting from horizon to horizon; but saw it now as the symbol of a vast power, huge, terrible, flinging the echo of its thunder over all the reaches of the valley, leaving blood and destruction in its path; the leviathan, with tentacles of steel clutching into the soil, the soulless Force, the iron-hearted Power, the monster, the Colossus, the Octopus.

—Frank Norris, 1901

And Geronimo was there, Leon. Pan-American Exposition. 1901. Fierce Geronimo. He was there. For real. Apache terror. Apache tears. In the Indian Village exhibit at the Pan-American Exposition. Three times a day, under special armed guard, he performed his own defeat with a cast of thousands.

Geronimo, Leon. Geronimo!

Bang, bang, you're dead.

OK. So what happened next? You had your break-down in 1898, Leon. You were crazy. Damn telephone ringing all the time. And Emma. Emma Goldman. Red Emma. (*Mother Earth*, Free Love, and the Revolution.) You stupid idiot. You went to see her, didn't you?

Yeah. That's what you did, and you jabbered like an idiot at her. Because you're stupid, Leon. Simple. You can't even hold a job. Can't even look your stepmother in the eye when she berates you. Oh Jeeze! A brick short of a full load. And what did you call yourself? Nieman, wasn't it? Fred Nieman. You told her your name was Fred Nieman. And Nieman in some eastern European language means "nobody." Fred Nobody.

Oh, Leon. Your real mother is dead. She died a long time ago when you were a boy in Detroit. Leon. Oh, Leon. Do not be sad. You break my heart, brother. There is a whole other America weeping for you to-night. Motherless children, all. And the boys with no faces.

Nobody.
But the funny thing is, Leon. Ha, ha, ha. Laugh out loud. They thought you were a spy. Emma and the others. The anarchists. They thought you were a spy. They listened to your wild and keening nullity. Your American sorrow. And they thought you were a spy.
Even wrote you up in the September 1, 1901 issue of Free Society. "The attention of the comrades is called to another spy. He is well-dressed, of medium height, rather narrow-shouldered, blond, and about twenty-five years of age." They said your demeanor was of "the usual sort, pretending to be greatly interested in the cause, asking for names, or soliciting aid for acts of contemplated violence." They said that you had already appeared in Chicago and Cleveland, and that if you showed up anywhere else... anywhere else... anywhere else, Mr. Nobody... "the comrades are warned in ad-

vance, and can act accordingly."

Five days later you shot President William McKinley twice in the stomach in the Temple of Music at the Pan-American Exposition in Buffalo. And you laid him in his grave.

The simplest Surrealist act consists of dashing down into the street, pistol in hand, and firing blindly, as fast as you can pull the trigger, into the crowd. Anyone who, at least once in his life, has not dreamed thus putting an end to the petty system of debasement and cretinization in effect has a well-defined place in that crowd, with his belly at barrel level.

—Andre Breton, 1930

Well, you got what you wanted, didn't you Leon? And you surely accomplished what you set out to do. Jesus Christ, Leon! Just tell me this. Just tell me one thing? How does it feel? How does it feel? To arrest history in one moment? And stop nothing?

Of course, they beat the shit out of you, Leon. Secret Service agents. After gunshots like outrageous knockings of ghostly radiators had shattered the clock and freed time. And you shouting stupid, illiterate things like, "I done my duty! I done my duty!" And they were smashing you in the face again and again. And you shouting, "I am a disciple of Emma Goldman!" And the fury of the nation. Smash! Smash! Smash! Unleashed now in such ghostly industrial howls and animal noises, until it is not clear whether the keening is coming from you or from them or from the blood-stained ground of this the last and the best of the Promised Lands—and neither does it matter Leon, neither does it matter. The American century is calling. The American century is calling. Piston, pump, pulse the screech of steel on steel. O my sad Americans at the turn of the century. Lost in great vast industrial no man's lands until John Henry drops his hammer and fucking dies. Just fucking dies.

It's too funny, Leon. Too fucking funny.

So they gave you the chair. And they sent two different jolts of 1,700 volts of pure American optimism coursing through your body for a full minute of 60 seconds each time. And you know what? Today, nobody even remembers your name, Leon. You stupid, crazy mother-fucker.

Leon Czolgosz, a.k.a. Fred Nieman, aged 28. Nobody.

Oh, Leon. My brother. You break my heart.

The Ghosts of Laredo

"I see by your outfit that you are a cowboy"
These words he did say as I boldly stepped by,
"Come sit down beside me and hear my sad story,
I was shot in the breast and I know I must die."
—"The Streets of Laredo (Cowboy's Lament)"

October 22, 1934. Ellen Conkle's farm outside Clarkson, Ohio. A man sits in a car, waiting to make his get-away. The owner of the car is shucking corn on the farmhouse porch. The man waiting in the car has decided not to steal it. He's been running for years now, this man waiting in the still car. Running his whole life. On the lam. He's a bandit. An outlaw. But he has decided not to steal the car because these are good people. When the owner of the car is finished with the chores, he'll help the fugitive make his get-away, help him get back to his running.

Back in 1925 the man in the car had left the King Cotton fields of the Cookson Hills out in Oklahoma. Out there where Jesse and Frank. Where Cole and the others. Henry Starr. Out where the desperate and the hungry lived and operated and hid out—Indian Territories—out there—where the desperate and hungry were seeking succor and refuge from the galloping and grabbing of the banks and the railroad men—and don't forget their lackeys, the laws and the Pinkertons, neither—out there seeking refuge from the ten thousand forces of carpetbagger-robber-baron capital and greed, seeking refuge from what would come to consciousness as Mr. Norris' Octopus, refuge from what would make the Wobblies rage and Big Bill Haywood bellow, refuge from that great fat-cat beast sucking down every inch of land and every reason-to-live, sucking down all grand dreams of finally you, yourself, mattering under the sun which also rises over the common man and woman of this great Republic.

So the man had left the hills and cotton fields of Sallisaw, Oklahoma, and lit out for St. Louis. Lit out, just like Jesse James or even Jimmie Rodgers, the "Singing Brakeman," for something different than share-cropping like his Daddy did before him, for the promise of city lights and silk shirts and selling bootleg whiskey. Lit out for walking down the street with head held high and shoulders not slumped even when it was real cold. But it hasn't always been like that, has it Pretty Boy? Hasn't always been the case that a proud-but-poor boy like yourself, a back-country bootlegging boy like yourself, coming into town maybe once every two months, could hold his head up high on such small town streets like those of Sallisaw. (And now, you're going back in time, and it's Christmastime, and you're just a kid again, and your name is Charles Arthur Floyd, but every buddy calls you Choc because you're fond of choc beer even now at this age, and you're out buying presents for the family. All the would-be city-slicker-swells of Sallisaw, these small-town sophisticates, have store-bought clothes and coats, and you don't, and so you're cold and humiliated, and your older brother even fought over there in the War to End All Wars and saw Gay Pah-ree, and still they laugh and sneer as you pass by.) When you were a kid. A greenhorn. A farm boy. Lit out, brother. Just lit out, didn't you, Pretty Boy? You'll show them someday. Show yourself. Make a name for yourself. In America. Someday.

And he's been running ever since.

Now he's waiting in the car for its owner to finish shucking corn and give him a ride, 'cause he's cracked up his wheels in an unmoored and crazy and bloody chase, and his partner is already taken if not yet dead.

A ride elsewhere. Not even St. Louis. Doesn't even have to be Chi-town. Just elsewhere. Get me the fuck outta here. One more ride, pretty as you please, out of the jaws of the inevitable, until some other day—just not today, please—until some other day, you meet your Maker and a bullet in the back and stop your running forever.

Man, he's just waiting.

But now its over sixty years later, and I don't know why this is happening to me.

Me in particular.

Don't know why I see this man. Why over sixty years later I see this man waiting to make his one last great dash.

I see him. Sitting there in that car just waiting until the chores get done before he can find some safety. Some cover. 'Cause chores always come first, don't you know? Even before the need to not be caught out in the open when the G-men have named you Public Enemy Number One; and Melvin Purvis himself is on your trail; and Dillinger has already gone down in an alley next to the Biograph in Chicago; and Bonnie and Clyde, too, caught somewhere in an ambush down south (and later, though you won't know it, Pretty Boy, because you're dead, the car Bonnie and Clyde were killed in will draw even more crowds then the car President Kennedy—that Catholic, that Irishman in the land of Know-Nothings and the Ku Klux Klan— even more than that car President Kennedy was riding in when they got him, too—though I think that this latter gunning down might be a little different than the ones we are presently contemplating from the study of a manse in New York)—but anyway, to get back to what we were saying, chores always come first in God's green world, even when the jig is up and the G-men are closing in and you're hot and got to move fast—and brother, that ain't no lie.

But like I say, I see this man in the car. And its over sixty years later. And I see him quite often, here in the manse—like a ghost that just don't know it's not real anymore. And he's still waiting. Like a ghost that don't know it can go home—don't even know that it's not my ghost, that it's not me it ought to be haunting, because I am an educated man and do not even believe in ghosts and besides don't have the words to explain just how it is that this man could actually finally quit waiting and go on to his rest. No sir. Don't have the words, because America has already forgotten him and his kind and his people, and without memory there's nothing left in America but running and waiting and haunting. In this land of Horatio Alger. In this America. And so we become them. Forever. Cops and Robbers alike. Ghosts.

So what I'm saying is I have no idea just what the deal is here. But I see this man a lot. And I think about the tyranny of rhythms. Corn gotta be shucked. I think about the tyranny of earth's deep cycles. You ain't never gonna beat the rhythm of the land. (So beat the drum slowly.) And even I know that, even out here in New York City. (And play the fife lowly.) And when crops gotta come in. And when the corn gotta be shucked. Well, it don't matter if you're Pretty Boy Floyd, trying to make one more spectacular escape. Don't matter nohow. Chores gotta get done.

And so the man is waiting. And the man has decided not to steal the car because these are good people. People like us. Just folks.

Then beat the drum slowly and play the fife lowly,
Beat the Dead March as you carry me along,
We all love our cowboys so young and so handsome,
We all love our cowboys although they've done wrong.

We all want to ride, don't we? We all still, somehow, want to make a name for ourselves in America. And 'tis a truesure wonderment what we will do just to see ourselves on TV. Me, myself—I, who should know better on account of my good education—I, too, still want to find that last great claim in the Klondike, that last Lost Mine in Colorado, that Great Rock Candy Mountain. I, too, want to light out for to find what the whole shebang always seems to be promising but never quite fulfilling.

And I, too, want to find someone to blame. I am not a violent man, but can quite easily imagine myself gunning down Leviathan in broad daylight and riding for the hills with great glee and gasps of gratitude.

Becoming one more ghost. One more outlaw. Fugitive. One more Cain-kid on the outlaw trail, always waiting to make my get-away. Trapped in history. In Gravity. Being crushed under the heel of the tyranny of cycles. Of rhythms. Of laws I cannot change.

Take me to the green valley and lay the sod o'er me
For I'm a young cowboy and I know I've done wrong.

And you too, Dear Reader, maybe you've longed for the purity of merely going from point A to point B, of actually getting to where you are going—or actually getting anywhere at all, instead of always returning to where you have always been. Maybe you, too, have longed to shatter orbits and careen in straight lines.

Pretty Boy. He wanted to be elsewhere. Wanted to rise up and over. Wanted to shake the cotton dust from his overhauls and maybe dance with a pretty little lady free from calluses on her pretty pink hands. Kill the curse. And return to some original St. Louis, if not Eden.

Yeah, well…

The fat-cats got their wants too. And they got guns.

October 22, 1934. Ellen Conkle's farm outside of Clarkson, Ohio. A man waiting to make his get-away.

Sitting in a car waiting to return to running. But now there are cars coming from all over the place, and their ain't no time for waiting. Ain't no time for chores. And the man takes off running. He is running across the field, 'cause they're sworn to take him dead or alive, but everybody knows they'd just as soon bring him in cold. Stiff. Dead. And so it's just one last sprint. One last straight line across the field. One last attempt to shatter orbits. One last attempt to reach the virgin timber on the other side of the fields, the other side of the curse, the other side of the Fall.

But there is a sharp crack and a falling, and the man is falling, forever falling, shot in the back, trapped pointblank in the falling of history, the plowing under of history, the returning to the same old story of history, the cycle of forgetting and returning, forgetting and returning to the dust from which we came, returning and forgetting and always waiting to return to running.

They are standing over the man. The laws. They are standing over the man with Winchester rifles. "Are you 'Pretty Boy'?" the G-man asks.

"I'm Charles Arthur Floyd," he says.

"Yeah, but you're 'Pretty Boy' right?"

"I'm Charles Arthur…"

"That's what I'm saying, you're 'Pretty Boy'…"

And then he's dead. A man without his name. A man condemned to become a ghost, who never made it to the virgin timber across the field, though he made it to Public Enemy Number One. A man haunting all us sad Americans who have no memory, who cannot give peace nor rest because we cannot remember, because we are stranded in the forever present and so seem to have become the pawn of the past—all us never-say-die Americans who must forever refuse to bury the dead because, in the end, it is we, the living, who haunt the dead, who rudely refuse them rest in our repeating of their refusals of deeper inevitables, in our forgetting, in our refusal to hear the one true lesson of the dead: that it is we who keep them from their last great escape—which after all, just might be, to surrender to the inevitability of deeper cycles, of deeper rhythms. Deeper even than the inevitability of chores or the inevitability of injustice. And then to fall. And in falling to such inevitables, to rise again, like the seed buried in the earth and bursting forth into gracious skies. A candle extinguished, and so forever lit. At last.

And to finally and definitively not be there. But here.

Oh muffle your drums, then play your fifes merrily
Play the Dead March as you go along
And fire your guns right over my coffin,
There goes an unfortunate boy to his home.

Frederick (All She Wrote)

1

Frederick was 92. Frederick was a mean son of a bitch. He'd always been that way, now and at the hour of his death. He'd stabbed himself twice in the stomach. He'd slashed at his wrists inconclusively. He was still a son of a bitch.

It's like this: Frederick was terminal and wanted to go. He found the most spiteful way. Let his daughter find him. And he made her clean up his mess one more time. And he made her clean up his mess.

When they took him off the respirator, I watched him die. I watched him die because it is part of what I do.

I stroked his forehead. It was scabby and obscene. I caressed him.

His mouth was dentureless. Spit and blood coagulated in the corners. I wiped it off.

And I said, "God is merciful." And knew it to be true.

And I said, "It's OK, you can go, we'll hold the fort." And that was true too.

And I rubbed his shoulders. And I caressed his arms. Swollen and weeping arms. I was his daughter's pastor. World without end. Swollen and weeping without end.

And it's like this: It takes much longer than you

would expect. There are a lot of false starts. And it happens in stages. But finally the son of a bitch died. And man, we didn't have anything to say, me and the family he hurt so bad.

But it was so peaceful. So very peaceful. Now and at the hour.

2

Well, one thing's certain. That's all she wrote, Frederick. Slow morphine drip. The graceful descent of a well-built paper airplane. And then you're gone. Yes sir, Frederick. All the rest of us poor sons of bitches should be so lucky. Now and at the hour of our death. Yeah.

But there's one thing Frederick: I, who caressed your swollen and weeping arms, though you were nothing to me but one of our own—and that really is sufficient, isn't it?—will never comprehend the human heart. Because in your frailty even your daughter, who was afraid of elevators, and never knew her grace in your gaze, forgave you; though at the last, her pen ripped the paper, the paper that released you and said it was OK to go home now into great white eternity, to go home now though you had never released her, or even once in her life made her feel pretty like only a Daddy can because, Frederick, you were a mean son of a bitch, and like I said, the pen ripped the paper and at the hour of your death ink stained her hands, so that at the end even her love got stained, and embraces were awkward when the doctors came back and gently encouraged us to leave and you were dead leaving her with so many questions and a grief and a guilt and a withered life left to mourn. And she still forgave you. And you never even said thank you.

Frederick, I do not comprehend the human heart. Either its frailties or its capacity to endure. Or its courage.

But I did your funeral. Because someday somebody will do mine. All us poor sons of bitches. All us poor children. Amen.

Jeremiad
(Mill Girls of 1912)

That's the Rebel Girl, That's the Rebel Girl.
To the working class, she's a precious pearl.
She brings Courage, Pride and Joy
To the fighting Rebel Boy.
Joe Hill, "Rebel Girl", 1915

I dream the women of Lawrence, marching arm in arm, beneath the Stars and Stripes, singing Joe Hill songs just like everything is jake. 1912. Massachusetts. Wobblies. One Big Union. I dream the mill girls of Lawrence, mothers and daughters that someone loved and needed, marching the picket lines—joyous, triumphant, free. Strike! Strike! Damn fat cats—damn Billy Wood and his ilk—want to cut wages by 32 cents a week in the textile mills in Lawrence in 1912. Something about the tariff. Something about the 54 hour work week. "Short pay! Short pay!" Four loaves of bread.

That's what 32 cents bought you in Lawrence, Massachusetts in 1912, when they walked out of the mills and said, "I just ain't going to take it no more"; when they said, "My baby needs milk"; when they decided that this time it was going to matter—yessir—this one's for all the pretty girls with missing fingers—this one's for all the beatings at the hands of men you love who have been brought to their knees like dogs—preach it!—this one's for every mill girl knocked up by a supervisor who does it because he can—O my sweet Jesus, he just can—this one's for every old-country family root ripped out in the long passage across the Atlantic—O the mothers! O the fathers!—because, well, you know—gotta get a job—this one's for every miscarriage and infant death by starvation in this the land of opportunity and Horatio Alger—every disappointment swallowed—every promise broken, every fucking lifelong humiliation as if your very birth were a curse. Yessir. This one's for you, they said. Women of Lawrence. 1912. The eyes of the world are upon you.

They walked out. They stood up. For two months and two days. Fucking immigrants. Kikes and wops and bohunks. They were Americans. And we've all but forgotten them in our republic of images.

And Jesus, didn't we want to stop them in 1912? We, Americans. Didn't we want to bring out the militia, the soldiers, the guns? Got a good thing going in this America. Got a bona fide middle class. We got farmers who can read. We got merchants and local shop owners. We got Main Street and elm trees. We got shareholders. In this proper America. But you ain't going to see that in Lawrence. And you ain't going to see that in no mining camp in Idaho.

Man, get with the program, it's 1912 and the niggers down south are in their place. Lynch law rules.

Jim Crow surely done good after Reconstruction. Got it under control. We got new troubles now. It's a new day in America, children. 1912. We got the Catholics. We got the corporations. We got the immigrants. We got all that cheap labor that makes the world go round. And don't you forget, we're a world power, baby. Great White Fleet. It's an industrial revolution. You don't mess with success. You don't mess with Capital.

Oh, they built the ship Titanic to sail the ocean blue,
And they thought they had a ship that the water would never leak through,
But the Lord's almighty hand knew that ship would never stand.
It was sad when the great ship went down.

(Chorus)
Oh, it was sad, so sad; it was sad, so sad;
It was sad when the great ship went down, to the bottom of the...
Husbands and wives, little children lost their lives,
It was sad when that great ship went down.

Oh, they sailed away from England, and were almost to the shore,
When the rich refused to associate with the poor,
So they put them down below, where they were the first to go.
It was sad when the great ship went down.

Oh they built another ship they called, "Titanic II."
They were sure this time that the water would never leak through.
So they launched it with a cheer, and it sank right off the pier.
It was sad when the great ship went down.
—William and Versey Smith, "The Titanic", 1927

And Big Bill Haywood. I dream that old son of a bitch too, that old cowboy, old homesteader, miner, rabble rouser, labor agitator, head breaker—Wob-

116

bly—true American—born in Salt Lake City, 1869. His daddy was a Pony Express rider—rode fast across an ancient landscape that did not acknowledge his presence even on moonlit nights when it was just him and the horse and all those cold stars like eyes that don't see you. You better believe it. Big Bill was the real thing, genuine article. Rootin' tootin' American from the Old Time West where fed up Mormons killed settlers in Mountain Meadows and blamed it on the Indians and Chief Joseph of the Nez Perce said, "I will fight no more forever," after the soldiers caught him and his small band, before they could slip across the Canadian border to freedom in 1887. Manifest destiny.

Yessir. I dream Big Bill Haywood in 1912. He came to Lawrence. He came by train sometime after the mill bosses planted dynamite in tenements and tried to get the coppers to believe that it was the I.W.W.—Industrial Workers of the World—Wobblies—cuz everybody knows those bastards are dynamite crazy—sabotage!—ride the rails—ain't got no home—buncha vags—buncha layabouts—lying, thieving bastards wouldn't do a days work if you paid them—always going on about their rights and free speech and taking over the means of production for the ones that actually do the work—always blaspheming against Jesus, property and apple pie—against everything that makes a manful man tear up when Old Glory passes in parade and we sure as hell whipped those greasy Spaniards in Cuba in 1898—those monkeys in the Philippines—when our soldiers—our brave boys in blue—roamed the islands in 1899 and just fucking slaughtered them in numbers you wouldn't believe.

McKinley called for volunteers,
Then I got my gun,
First Spaniard I saw coming
I dropped my gun and run,
It was all about that Battleship of Maine.

(Chorus)
At war with that great nation Spain,
When I get back to Spain I want to honor my name,
It was all about that Battleship of Maine.

Why are you running?
Are you afraid to die?
The reason that I'm running
Is because I cannot fly,
It was all about that Battleship of Maine.

When they were a-chasing me,
I fell down on my knees,
First thing I cast my eyes upon
Was a great big pot of peas,
It was all about that Battleship of Maine.

The peas they were greasy,
The meat it was fat,
The boys was fighting Spaniards
While I was fighting that,
It was all about that Battleship of Maine.
Traditional, "The Battleship of Maine"

118

Yessir. Big Bill came to Lawrence in 1912 to help organize the strike because they arrested Giovannitti and Ettor—leaders of the strike—arrested them for murder when a girl got shot in some melee with the militia even though they were both a mile a way and didn't have a damned thing to do with it. Conspiracy or some such hogwash. Inciting violence. I don't know. They just wanted to break the strike—wanted to cut it off at the head—the bosses and the shareholders and all those law and order types who got fat on the backs of labor—decent men like you and me and Big Bill Haywood...

Well, maybe not like Big Bill. Wasn't he a terrorist? Wasn't he some kind of Red? I mean, he was banging his sister-in-law when the cops nabbed him in 1906—I mean, he was actually doing that when they nabbed him—and took him back to Idaho under cover of night in a special train arranged for just this caper so it wouldn't have to stop at all and give the Wobblies a chance to spring him—cuz it wasn't exactly legal kidnapping him like that without an extradition hearing, but you just don't play nicey nice with terrorists, boys. You just don't.

Yeah, they arrested Big Bill in 1906 because ole Harry Orchard turned stool pigeon when he got nabbed for planting a bomb in the former governor of Idaho's mailbox, blew the shit out of him, right there in front of his wife and daughter. Frank Steunenberg was his name. Guy who got offed for messing with the Western Federation of Miners. Yessir. Harry Orchard fingered Big Bill—said the order came down from the bosses of the WFM—so they took Big Bill back to Idaho and he was a hero to many. To the Other Half. Better believe it.

Clarence Darrow himself came out west and defended him in court in the Trial of the Century in 1906—and you're not going to believe this, but even got him off—got him off, so Big Bill could get back out there and Organize, Organize—don't mourn, boys!—get in the game, torch up the night—lead the Children home to the Promised Land.

Did he do it? Did he do it? Did he order the hit on Governor Steunenberg in America at the turn of the century after Haymarket, after Homestead, after Pullman? Hell yeah, he did it. And plenty more.

I dream Big Bill Haywood with his one blind, milky-dead, eye, towering over the people, singing slogans—talking bull—telling tales.

Long-haired preachers come out every night,
Try to tell you what's wrong and what's right;
But when asked how 'bout something to eat
They will answer in voices so sweet:

You will eat, bye and bye,
In that glorious land above the sky;
Work and pray, live on hay,
You'll get pie in the sky when you die

Workingmen of all countries, unite

Side by side we for freedom will fight
When the world and it's wealth we have gained
To the grafters we'll sing this refrain:

You will eat, bye and bye,
When you've learned how to cook and how to fry;
Chop some wood, 'twill do you good
Then you'll eat in the sweet bye and bye
—Joe Hill, "The Preacher and the Slave", 1911

•

I dream the women of Lawrence. I dream the winter of 1912. Coldest winter in memory. I dream the fire hoses turned on the women without mink stoles and furs. Frigid water and your hair freezes. I dream the hunger and the want—the fact of mothers weighing the need to stand up, to claim their right to be here—because no one is going to hand it to you, sister—claim their worthiness of both bread and roses—O give me roses—give me roses—weigh it against the starving of the children, the waning and wasting of the children. It's grim, my fellow Americans. I'm telling you. It's grim. Every day they march the picket lines—can't arrest you for vagrancy if you are moving on, always moving on—and every day they face the bayonets of the militia. Local boys, farm boys, boys out on a lark, pressed into duty that is not clear or clean. They do not hate you so much as play the cards dealt.

"Hey baby, baby. Won't you make an appointment with me?"

"I'm sorry, dear sir, but I only date men."

The women; some of them young, smitten and in love. Defiant and alive. Pregnant in their shirtwaists. They are the backbone of the strike. They do not falter when their men crumple in weakness and rage. They stand up. The women of Lawrence. They pool resources. Peel donated potatoes for the great soup kitchens sustaining the strikers. Bake pizzas for the neighborhood. Bread for the people. I dream the women; their gut level determination. Their sacrifice and their guilt. The tenderness. The giddiness. The fact of their children not having enough to eat.

If you all will shut your trap,
I will tell you 'bout a chap,
That was broke and up against it too, for fair;
He was not the kind to shirk,
He was looking hard for work,
But he heard the same old story everywhere:

(Chorus)
Tramp, tramp, tramp, keep on a-tramping,
Nothing doing here for you;
If I catch you 'round again,
You will wear the ball and chain,
Keep on tramping, that's the best thing you can do.

Down the street he met a cop,
And the copper made him stop,
And he asked him, "When did you blow into town?
Come with me up to the judge,"

But the judge he said, "Oh fudge,
Bums that have no money needn't come around."

Finally came that happy day
When his life did pass away,
He was sure he'd go to heaven when he died,
When he reached the pearly gate,
Santa Peter, mean old skate,
Slammed the gate right in his face and loudly cried:
—Joe Hill, "The Tramp", 1913.

I dream the women of Lawrence. And the desperation. What to do about the children? Everyday, it's the same. They march the pickets, they take their shift. And then they come home and take their turn at caring for the babes. Neighborhood babes. Little ones. Wee ones. The babes....but they don't look like babes. Do they? The little ones. They look like tiny old men. Miniature old women. The mills take away your youth—your innocence. Make you old. The little ones. With eyes that seem to look right through you. Jesus gonna make up my dyin' bed. Jesus gonna make up my dyin' bed. And they are so hungry. Just ain't ever enough to eat. I don't care how many bowls of thin charity soup you get down at Franco-Belgian Hall. Hunger prowls like a wild beast. Hunger walks on two feet like a man. Lawlessness and bloodlust just a flashing eye away.

So the Wobblies—they figured they had a plan. Advertised in all the Socialist papers. All the Anarchist papers. Looking for good folks to take the kids the duration of the strike. Send them out of harm's way.

And the response is overwhelming. Offers came from all over. The eyes of America are upon you, Lawrence.

The eyes are upon you, mothers of Lawrence, as you march your children to the train station. And it's breaking your hearts. And you are having second thoughts. And you are just sure that this ache is going to kill you. It hurts. It hurts. More than any bayonet or insolent bossman. To surrender your babes. To send them off to the care of strangers. One Big Union. We are all brothers. All sisters. We must be brave, mothers of Lawrence. We must be brave.

Aw jeeze. Not a dry eye at the station. Make a grown man turn his face. To see the courage of the mothers. The sacrifice of the mothers. One last hug. Clutch to the breast. And then gone. Gone. Onto trains bound to places where they can't hurt you now. They can't hurt you now. Boston! New York! O my children, you are going on a great adventure. Great Rock Candy Mountain. All you can eat and the streets are paved with butter. Soon. Soon....

And then the return from the station. The return to cold tenements. Tenements without the children. The women of Lawrence. The helplessness of your man. And the humiliation of having to witness it. A good man. A good man. Shouldn't be this way. O my sweet Mother of God. It just fucking hurts. Grim. Aw jeeze. Resolve. There are strikers to be fed. Scabs to be jeered. We shall overcome. We shall overcome. Our love is greater than your guns. It just is.

I dream the mothers of Lawrence.

Thus says the LORD:
"For three transgressions of Judah, and for four,
I will not turn away its punishment,
Because they have despised the law of the LORD,
And have not kept His commandments.
Their lies lead them astray,
Lies which their fathers followed.
But I will send a fire upon Judah,
And it shall devour the palaces of Jerusalem."

Thus says the LORD:
"For three transgressions of Israel, and for four,
I will not turn away its punishment,
Because they sell the righteous for silver,
And the poor for a pair of sandals.
They pant after the dust of the earth which is on the head of the poor,
And pervert the way of the humble.
A man and his father go in to the same girl,
To defile My holy name.
They lie down by every altar on clothes taken in pledge,
And drink the wine of the condemned in the house of their god."
—Amos 2:4-8 (NKJV)

I dream the women of Lawrence and their outside agitators, foreign element, nosey, no-good Reds like Elizabeth Gurley Flynn, original Rebel Girl, blue-eyed Irish dazzler, the face of the strike—Lord, how that woman could talk—and didn't she look smart up there on a podium?—tiny compared to Big Bill, but with a heart the size of Texas, the size of the twentieth century, the size of America. She escorted the children of Lawrence on their great adventure. Took them to New York where they were greeted with cheers, with jeers. Led them on a march down Fifth Avenue, the little kiddies holding signs:

"A Little Child Shall Lead Them."

"They Asked for Bread, They Received Bayonets."

"We Never Forget."

Fifth Avenue is lined with cheering supporters, factory workers, sympathetic mothers, wealthy socialites with bad consciences and a grudge against father. With jeers. Fifth Avenue is lined with enraged capitalists and shop clerks just a paycheck away from poverty, meanness, millwork, screaming at the kiddies, spit flying. The battle lines are drawn. The fault lines are exposed. We are cracking up in America. We are coming apart. And the eyes of the world are upon us.

And Margaret Sanger, rebel of the female body, author of "What Every Girl Should Know," scourge of that old puritan Anthony Comstock, is there too—New York City—working as a nurse, examining the children when they arrive at the station. And what does she see? And what does she find? There is malnutrition in our America—there is rickets. Premature aging. A little girl with a bald spot from when her hair was caught in the works and her scalp ripped off and they rushed her to the hospital and were able to sew it back on so she would live, but would never be pretty again, never let down her hair again, never flip her hair again, when alone among the mill girls after the men have all gone—without remembering. Home of the brave. The eyes of the world are upon you, Lawrence and they see your children. They see what the industrial revolution does to children. Your wizened, starving children. And they hate you for it, Lawrence. They blame you for it, Lawrence.

As we go marching, marching, in the beauty of the day,
A million darkened kitchens, a thousand mill lofts gray,
Are touched with all the radiance that a sudden sun discloses,
For the people hear us singing: Bread and Roses! Bread and Roses!

As we go marching, marching, we battle too for men,
For they are women's children, and we mother them again.
Our lives shall not be sweated from birth until life closes;
Hearts starve as well as bodies; give us bread, but give us roses.

As we go marching, marching, we bring the greater days,
The rising of the women means the rising of the race.
No more the drudge and idler, ten that toil where one reposes,
But a sharing of life's glories: Bread and roses, bread and roses.

Our lives shall not be sweated from birth until life closes;
Hearts starve as well as bodies; bread and roses, bread and roses.
    —James Oppenheim, "Bread and Roses", 1911

The city fathers are enraged. The city fathers are appalled. The city fathers will not stand for this. Boosters of Lawrence. All this bad publicity. They are portraying our fair city as if it were Tsarist Russia. Our American city. Lawrence is a model city. City on a hill. This is just anarchist propaganda. The papers, the rags, sensationalist journalism! God damn Wobblies must be stopped. The eyes of the world are upon us. The eyes of the world are upon us.

And Mayor Scanlan. He's up against it too. You know

how much it is costing the city of Lawrence to have the militia here? Who do you think has to pay for that? And the cops—well, the papers are just reaming them. Suggesting they can't cut it. Suggesting that the cops are hiding behind the militia. Something's got to give. Something's got to give.

And the kiddies are sending letters home. Home from New York, home from Boston. Home from the diaspora. And the letters are finding their way into the papers. The kiddies are amazed to be free to play. Free to go to school. Free to go to bed with full stomachs. This isn't good. A regular PR nightmare. Makes it look like the mill owners of Lawrence are a pack of monsters, pack of misers, pack of fatcats grinding the children of Lawrence beneath the heel of the Almighty Dollar—unholy Mammon!—and for all practical purposes, this is Victorian America—this is Christian America—this is the birth of childhood—and advertising—this is still the time when Little Nell makes sense—things can't go on like this anymore. Something's got to give.

So when the Wobblies began to organize another exodus, the die was cast. Moods were grim. The cops had something to prove. They were not going to let those babes get on the train.

No. Not this time.

"And I will show wonders in the heavens and in the earth:
Blood and fire and pillars of smoke.
The sun shall be turned into darkness,
And the moon into blood,
Before the coming of the great and awesome day of the

LORD."
—Joel 2:30-31 (NKJV)

I dream the women of Lawrence, clutching their children, parading down the street to the train station. I dream their men walking by their sides, determined, courageous, aggrieved. I dream the cops of Lawrence, they got their billy clubs, they got their guns—they got something to prove. The air is thick with steam and smoke from the train, from the locomotive—coal smoke from the mouth of the iron horse, iron dragon. O turn away! Turn away! But no, there is no turning away. You can smell the blood. I will not back down. I am an American. The women approach. They do not stop. A warning is given. Halt! Halt! They do not stop. Halt! Halt!. They do not halt. And all hell breaks loose.

Clubs are swung. Arms. Necks. Heads are cracked. O women of Lawrence! Jack booted thugs. Pregnant women shoved hard and thrown to the ground. Punched. Slapped. Stomped. This will show them! Scum! Immigrants! All the rage of nearly two months released in a bloody spasm. All the rage. The screams! The screams! Children are snatched from loving arms and tossed into paddy wagons like sacks of potatoes. Women cling to their babes. Shelter them with their thin, cold bodies. Claws scratch at cop-eyes. Blood on the street. The men roaring and impotent. You can hear the billy clubs sucking wind. O America! O America!

And the eyes of the world are upon you.

It wasn't supposed to be this way. In the republic of

129

images.

*Now the only way to avoid this shipwreck, and to pro-
vide for our posterity, is to follow the counsel of Micah,
to do justly, to love mercy, to walk humbly with our God.
For this end, we must be knit together, in this work, as
one man. We must entertain each other in brotherly affection. We must be willing to abridge ourselves of our
superfluities, for the supply of other's necessities.... We
shall find that the God of Israel is among us, when ten of
us shall be able to resist a thousand of our enemies; when
He shall make us a praise and glory that men shall say of
succeeding plantations, "may the Lord make it like that
of New England." For we must consider that we shall be
as a city upon a hill. The eyes of all people are upon us.
So that if we shall deal falsely with our God in this work
we have undertaken, and so cause Him to withdraw His
present help from us, we shall be made a story and a by-
word through the world.... We shall shame the faces of
many of God's worthy servants, and cause their prayers
to be turned into curses upon us till we be consumed out
of the good land whither we are going.*
    —Gov. John Winthrop, "A Model of Christian
Charity", 1630

O my America.

*Hear this word that the LORD has spoken against you,
O children of Israel, against the whole family which I
brought up from the land of Egypt, saying:*

130

"You only have I known of all the families of the earth;
Therefore I will punish you for all your iniquities."
A lion has roared!
Who will not fear?
The Lord GOD has spoken!
Who can but prophesy?
—Amos 3:1-2, 8 (NKJV)

I dream the women of Lawrence and how they kept the peace that day. Love and Self-Control. The men wandered the streets for hours howling in rage and impotence. Shots were fired, but no one was killed. That day. Yeah. For all intents and purposes they won the strike that day.

Newspaper men were there. Reporters. The eyes of the world. America was brought to her knees. We are not like this. This is not who we are. The mill owners caved. The strikers got their 32 cents and a little more. They stood up.

They just stood up.

I dream the women of Lawrence. They were Americans. I think I smell smoke.

George

George is a crotchety old man. George is the father of Ms. Mary and her sister. My father-in-law. And George is terminal. They can't deal with the cancer because of the heart, and they can't deal with the heart because of the cancer. So he's going to die. Or better, because George is a good Catholic, he's going home. He's eighty. "I'm doomed," he says, "Aw, what the hell..."

The family sent me on a mission here to Chicagoland—I'm back on the prairie of my origins—to take care of George because Ms. Mary's sister is dealing with the chemo for her third recurrence of breast cancer (it's in the spine now) and can't travel, and because Ms. Mary was here for a month and today they started demolishing our kitchen for the eight week remodel (apparently they found an old fireplace where the stove used to be), and besides she was going a little crazy out here in the land of ranch houses, parking lots, blond brick, and flatlands—and because I'm a Minister and today the Oncologist was going to try and make it clear again to George that he is terminal. Stage four cancer. Four to six months to live.

So today, the long and short of it is that George got it that he was going to die. You could see it happen. He's a proud man. WWII vet. So it wasn't like you were going to see an opera. George just got it. We went home. I made hamburgers. He drank a big glass of wine. Had a beer. (Why not?) Fell asleep on the couch.

George owns a ranch house in the south suburbs of Chicago. Just outside of Kankakee. Not too far from Joliet. When he bought the place 25 or 30 years ago there were 3500 people in town. Now there's over nine thousand. A bunch of them drive BMWs, and they live in the lonesomest mansions—each on a hill that exists only metaphorically. Traffic is a nightmare. He doesn't go to any of the new restaurants. He likes Klaus', where you can get a pint and a schnitzel.

Anyway, when George bought the place, there was just a crawl space beneath the house. Well, damned if he didn't dig out a basement beneath the foundation, bucketful by bucketful—had a neighbor kid to help him—and built a finished basement. I'm sitting in it now. And in his basement he installed a workshop where he built his own violins. I shit you not. Glued them together, varnished them, did it all—and he built a model railroad on a huge platform with switches and bridges and big ole cigar ashes on the floor.

George grew up in Cleveland, and he still thinks of it as home although he told me today that he thought that was odd considering how he only lived there 18 years. After that, he got drafted. He was on his way to Japan when they dropped the bomb on Hiroshima. On Nagasaki. Didn't see a day of fighting. He seems pleased as punch about that. Tickles him pink. Like he got one over on the sonsabitches. His younger brother signed up for Korea, and was worried that their Dad, who worked in the coal mines of Pennsylvania and still received Socialist and Commie literature in the mail, might be a problem for him... Goddamn bohunk!

Anyway, George is kind of grateful that I'm here, he says, because I don't tell him what to do, like the women. The women are Ms. Mary and her sister, who can both be kind of bossy. Reminds him of their mother, Ms. Alice. (Who I love also with a gratitude that I don't quite understand, though I can attest to her bossiness.) And George still loves her, too. And that's kind of sad—because she divorced him over twenty years ago. I gather they fought a bit. She wanted strange things. Bright Lights, Big City. And never did like to drink beer with the cousins in basements all night until morning came too soon and the boss was gonna be an asshole about it—although she did seem to love his violin playing. Wasn't George the concertmaster for the Kankakee Symphony for years? And didn't he own his own goddamn tux? I mean, he owned it, dammit.

George thinks it's OK that I'm a Protestant, although he seems to be a little nervous that my dad is Republican. Still—on the whole—he figures I'm a good guy. He lets me tell him when it's time to take his medicine, and he wanted me to be there when the doctor told him the bad news. He already knew the news, by the way. He's known it for a while. He just lets news be true—bad or good—on his own terms. He wanted me to be there, though, and I gotta say, I am grateful beyond words to be able to be a son in a way that my father would never let me be.

Not that my own father doesn't love me—he does, like water going downhill—it's just that my Dad understands his fatherhood differently. He and my mother moved to Idaho and quickly set up the deal for their latter days. They pay some kind of insurance money up front, and their care is secured at every stage until they just die. My sister and I will never ever have to wonder what to do about mom and dad. My sister and I will never be able to be daughters and sons in that way.

And so I gotta say, I'm grateful to George. Because I need to be a son in that way.

So he had his beer and his wine—and I cracked a Pabst Blue Ribbon or two—and we watched the History Channel (All Nazis! All the time!), and we bitched about the women, and we left crumbs on the counter, and we burped without excusing ourselves, and scratched ourselves, and it was a good night.

George is one of the heroes of this country.

I love my wife. And as some of you know, I have been having a bit of trouble with ghosts over the last year or so. But I don't think I would be frightened if George came to me after the fact and wanted to just pass the time. I love my blood family. Like water going downhill. But I am learning how to be a son and a brother with my in-laws—although I am terrified that I am going to be the one to have to permanently and finally take away George's car keys. No, I think I would be a little less lonely if George came and passed the time with me, after the fact. We could bitch about the women. And nurse a love for them that just won't never die.

Well, I was supposed to be home last Thursday, but

George went and started leaking blood from his rectum again. "Shit, I crapped my pants..." So back into the hospital he went. The nurses tell me that after I left the hospital, they found him on his hands and knees in the bathroom cleaning up the blood and shit from the bathroom floor when he just didn't make it in time. He still had the fucking tube up his nose going down into his stomach. I don't even know how he got to the toilet.

We got him home, though. But he wasn't the same. George is checking out. Disengaging. He mixes things up. Thought the Bears were in the Rose Bowl. He wanted watermelon but thought it was too expensive. "What the hell do you care? You got a license to live large," I said, and he smiled. Really got a kick out of that. Living large. Heh, heh. But he didn't eat more than a slice of the melon. Didn't even seem to care that the Bears lost. "What the hell, it's only a game."

I'm leaving tomorrow. We got the hospice all set up. And I've gotta get back. One of my parishioners lost her husband, and another just got diagnosed as terminal. They aren't going to do anything except fix up the arm she busted leaning too hard on the bannister. Damned thing snapped like a twig. She's a trooper though. Old Scots stock. I called her at the hospital, and she asked about my father-in-law and Ms. Mary. Didn't want to waste words on herself.

Tonight, knowing I'm leaving, George says to me, he says, "You know, Stanley,"—he calls me Stanley—"I had a dream about a month ago. I saw the star of Jesus in my left eye."

"Star of Jesus?" I said.

"Yeah, the star of his birth. It was in my left eye, and it woke me up, and when I tried to go back asleep and find it again, it was gone. I tried to find it... It was like an omen..."

"Maybe God is showing you the way home, George." I said. (Although each word felt like a lash of a whip on my own back.)

"Yeah, I'm gonna die."

"Or maybe you're just going to be born again into your new life—eternal life." He was quiet then. He liked that. (I wanted to smash things.) He'd asked me earlier if he would see his mother. I said, "Yeah." He was quiet then, too. (I wanted someone to pay.)

So we watched some more Court TV. And then when he was ready to go to bed, he said, "You know, the dishwasher won't stop. It just keeps running its cycle. It's all bust."

"Uh-huh."

"And when Mary and my brother were here, the garage door broke and the windshield on the car got cracked..."

"It's like your house is breaking down with you, George. Sympathy pains."

"Yeah." He liked that, too. Made him chuckle.

"Good night, George."

"Good night, Stanley."

I gotta go. Plane is going to leave tomorrow, and they need me back home. Family is coming Saturday, and then after they leave, Ms. Mary and her sister are coming in for a couple of days. He's got neighbors that love him, that are gonna check up on him.

He's fading fast though. I don't know that I'm going to see him alive again. He doesn't need me anymore. Others are coming.

But here's the thing. I've been real good. Charon ferrying him across. You do your duty. You get out of the way and let the fellow feeling flow through. Yeah. And then you want to break things. And smash things and just fucking keen. Like the coyotes out here. (You know, there really are coyotes out here. I heard them. On the Prairie at night. Didn't believe it at first. But yeah. Coyotes).

And you know what? Jesus really is just calling him home. And he really will see all the home-folks again. And there won't be any pain or sorrow, and every tear shall be dried. Amen.

And he is turning away from us and turning toward something else, and I don't want him to go. And I miss my Dad. I miss my Mom.

And I'm just all tied up in knots about it. Like water that's gotta go downhill and don't have a say in it. Not a mumbling word.

It is what it is. You just got to get out of the way.

Well, I'm back on the Prairie, just a few miles south of where I used to live, where way back in 1934 they gunned down Dillinger in that alley beside the Biograph theater in Chicago—on that night when he was looking good in his "gray slacks, black socks, red Paris garters, and white buckskin Nunn Bush shoes"—but this time, today, George, my father-in-law, is in a hospital bed in his den with diapers and an old tee shirt, stuck between two worlds, all hopped up on morphine—Man they aren't ever going to take me alive! Take that, copper!—and he's all gaped mouth because he lost his partial somewhere in the bedclothes—Got one foot on the platform, one foot on the train—and he's making wild, defiant gestures. He's having conversations with dead people. He's neither here nor there. I mean, he's nowheresville, man.

"George, are you in pain?"

"George, do you need your morphine?"

He's clutching at the bedclothes. He's grimacing.

He's reaching for things I can't see.

"George..."

Last night with his broken femur he tried to crawl out of bed, clawing at the bed railings, because there was a train accident, he said, and he had to get to the trolley so he could help—Cleveland in the 40's—but they never gave him a chance, all those laws and G-men and cycles of life. We had to hold him down, me and Ms. Mary. He reached for his pistol—he was struggling to get out—but the fix was in. Blown away in a filthy alley. And all the pretty ladies—Mary AuBuchon called today to say she loved him—dipped handkerchiefs in his blood that just pooled there in the alley beside the Biograph and dreamed of good time johnnies. But Dillinger is always already gone, boys. Out of range. You ain't getting out of this world alive, George. No sir.

Yeah, you can watch little Georgie making his mad dash. Little Georgie who played the violin in Cleveland when they beat up kids for hearing something they didn't. You can watch it happen in real time. And tonight, I swear I'd carry a cross, harbor a fugitive, and smuggle one more wooden gun into the Crown Point Jail if only George could just make it this time. One more escape. One more last breath. Just gone.

There is evidence of a terrible struggle. Jacob and the angel. You can watch peace being born. George is going out in style. He's going out on his own time. Like a man. Like a musician. Or a killer. It's enough to bring you to your knees. It's enough to make you believe. Hallelujah.

What is there to do but to bow at the passing of a living man? And to fear God? Mountains must tremble at such a moment. And surely there is great rejoicing in heaven. Little Georgie is coming home, boys.

Yeah. And all we get is this body. This body that lies twitching and drooling. This body that shits on itself and babbles stupidly. This thing that will be consumed and turned to ashes. This boat. This raft. This thing that we will find burnt and abandoned on the shore—like a salt and pepper shaker you find on the lawn after a tornado and the house is just gone. Just like the obscene corpse of John Dillinger lying in an alley beside the Biograph theater in 1934.

Yeah. Even so. They can shoot us in the back, George. They can pretend like we weren't ever here. And erase our names and write other names over ours, pretty as you please, as if the writing weren't indelible. All those laws and G-men and cycles of life. They can make out like a man never lived. Well, they can just kiss my ass, George. Because I was here. And I'm going to remember. It just can't end this way. There ought to be fireworks.

At 6:10 this morning, as the sun came up over the prairie, George passed. It was very quick. Three short breaths and he was gone. The birds were making a commotion.

REPUBLIC OF DREAMS

"The wind bloweth where it listeth, and thou hearest the sound thereof, but canst not tell whence it cometh, and whither it goeth..."
— John 3:8 KJV

"You know how to whistle don't you, Steve? You just put your lips together and blow."
— Lauren Bacall in "To Have and to Have Not", 1944

PROLOGUE

American Home

It used to be that you knew you were a real New Yorker when you spent a lot of time talking about getting out. The irony of claiming some kind of authentic New-York-ness by means of portraying the city as if it were something you could slough off, like a youthful affection for ridiculous Robert Wilson productions at the Brooklyn Academy of Music, went unrecognized.

New York was an affectation. A prop. A backdrop to your own movie. It wasn't a place. It was a location.

That's not the way it is now. New York is a place, all right. It's where people make their homes and raise their kids. It's where families gather on holidays. It's where people bury their dead. And packs of abandoned dogs gone feral roam the great necropolises of

Queens at night. Borough of cemeteries.

Seems I've got new eyes these days. A prospective New Yorker of all told, sixteen years. I've got new eyes. I see things. The tawdry meanness of Bush-era Manhattan. Times Square and Shopping. The trash and fences on Queens Boulevard. Dog fights in Jamaica.

This is an ugly city.

City of hare lips and cold sores. City of cheap perfume and stupid American Idol dreams. Pharmacists and herbalists. City of gray-hamburger diners and Starbucks. Fortune tellers and pole dancers. Vocational colleges and degrees in Psychology. City of immigrants and unspeakable and scandalous dreams of home—the way home could be—the way home ought to be. And the way home actually is.

City of flan and ox tail soup. City of garlic and meat pies.

City of the LIE and the BQE. City of on-ramps and off-ramps landing on neighborhoods like expeditionary forces. Sad concrete gardens. Pigeon shit. Overflowing trash cans reeking of ketchup and grease on the Grand Concourse. Handball courts. Strip clubs. Banquet Halls on Metropolitan Avenue. Sweet sixteen extravaganzas.

New York is a place. And it is ugly. It is the central fact of New York. Its ugliness. The concrete and trash. The smell of urine and moldy awnings. The fact of its complete indifference to the lives of its inhabitants.

New York. This place of glamor and lights. Lies and time-wasting exaggerations. This place of the eight million souls.

God, I hate it, like the stone resents gravity. And yet I bless it with every breath I take. This New York. This place where everyone I know is always already defeated—and yet keeps on, like a ghost that doesn't know it's dead yet. This place where every illusion is dangerous—and yet there is rejoicing behind the triple-locked apartment doors of Lefrak City.

This place where love is fierce and guarded. And generous. And candid.

Outside the city, the word is that New Yorkers are loud and obnoxious, rude. All of that is true of course, but there is a sweetness and naiveté to New Yorkers that maybe tourists don't get to see. You just don't cast pearls before swine.

I mean. I'm just saying. In the city you don't play the sucker. You don't parade what you got where it will get soiled and trampled. Eighty million grubby fingers. Sixteen million unwashed feet. But that doesn't mean that New Yorkers don't have a world of generosity behind the game face. Behind the barred windows.

This is a city of habitual cruelty and ugliness—and miraculously, those who endure it more often than not come out on the other side—not so much unscathed—as unbowed. I hate this city like I hate that my father is getting old—like a kite hates the hand that holds the string.

I hate this city until I find again and again that I love it—and that my love couldn't be half as true without the hate.

And that seems like something to pay attention to. In the place where I make my American home.

WIDE AWAKE DREAMS

I Had a Dream

I dreamed I saw Mr. Melville's Confidence Man alive as well as you or me. I saw Timothy Leary and Tom Sawyer. I saw Gov. Blagojevitch. And just over my shoulder Jimmy Swaggart was crying Real Tears. And Nixon was Rocking Out. To the Upbeat Stylings of Up With People. At the Superbowl Halftime. Of Silent Majority Dreams.

I saw the Star Spangled Banner like a Bleeding Tongue—Whiplashed Truths and Razor Blade Justice. Old Glory. Our Flag Was Still There.

I saw the Medicine Show Professor and the Circus Barker and Ain't-He-Dreamy-Pulpits in Nineteenth Century Brooklyn. And thought of John Edwards. I saw Sinister Magicians and the Yellow Menace. And thought of Max Headroom. I saw Billy Sunday box the Devil. ("You're going down, Satan!") I saw Sister Aimee come from the Sea like a Movie Goddess—the Immaculate Conception of Athena—Greta Garbo On The Half Shell. And I measured the width of Senator Craig's Stance. Yessir. It was like a Parade of Days. It was like the Masque of the Red Death. It was Cosa Nostra.

I saw it all.

I even saw the Thing That Lives In The Trees. The Thing That Does Not Love You.

I shot Irony in the Back and Paid My Dues to the

Nature Theater of Oklahoma. I ain't no Organization Man. I Can Take A Joke.

I saw it all. Yeah.

And I liked it. All this Freedom. All this terrifying Freedom. You Only Go Around Once In Life So You've Got To Grab For All The Gusto You Can. You Can Call Me "Ray". Two All Beef Patties, Special Sauce, Lettuce, Cheese, Pickles, Onions, On A Sesame Seed Bun. You Deserve A Break Today.

I liked it all. All these Impostors. These Poseurs. All these Americans. Going Faster Miles An Hour. In dreams.

God on Your Shoulder

I woke from a dream in which I was poking the corpse of God. I was sticking it with a knife. Prodding it. I was finding stuff out. Like I was a doctor or something. It was research.

While I was poking the corpse of God, God came and kind of hung over my shoulder.

"What you doing?" He said.

I said, "I'm poking God".

""Finding stuff out?"

"Pretty much."

He was getting heavy. Hanging over my shoulder. God was kind of heavy. I could barely stand. He was so heavy.

How the hell was I supposed to find stuff out with that kind of burden? And if you want to know the truth, the corpse was kind of starting to smell.

"Listen," I said. "If you're going to hang around,

146

I'm just not going to get anything done. You're kind of heavy. And I've got a lot of stuff to find out."

He just kind of shifted on my shoulder and settled in. There was an awkward silence.

"So, he's dead, right?" God said.

"Pretty much."

"Good riddance."

"You're telling me," I said.

We smiled. I mean, he was on my shoulder and I couldn't see his face. But I knew he smiled.

I kept poking it. The corpse. Trying to find stuff out.

"You want I should say a blessing or something?" God said.

"It couldn't hurt," I said.

So he did what he did. And so help me.

And then we just stood there. Him on my shoulder. Heavier than gravity. And we just looked at that poor body. And it had my father's face. That thing. And it had my face. That corpse. And it had the face of everyone I know and love. Like some internet slide show. The face of my sister. My mother.

It was pretty close to home.

"You need a moment?" He asked. "You need a second to get it together?"

"Yeah," I said.

Man, He was heavy. God on your shoulders.

"Take your time," He said. "I ain't going anywhere."

The room smelled of roses.

Bernadine

Sometime last week I watched a documentary called

"Weather Underground". It was about what you would expect. There was archival footage of a young and beautiful Bernadine Dorhn—she was cold and pure— the sexy ascetic—she was saying that when you lived in the most violent society known to history, nonviolence was not an option. If you didn't act, you were culpable. If you weren't violent, you were complicitous.

She was beautiful in her youth, her purity—like an ad for a convent. She was diseased. O rose, thou art sick. (Ascetic youth. Anorexic youth. Bulimic youth.) She glowed like a consumptive. Beautiful.

There was contemporary footage of her in Chicago as well, forty years later, and she still glowed, but now like ripening fruit. There was a stillness in her eyes—a patience, as if time had burned an image on her lenses. Something was frozen and maybe arrested. There was the smell of burning leaves and eyes that don't need to turn away—the smell of bombs—eyes that lock on without belligerence or provocation—but just look. She was beautiful.

You could set entire epics between those two clips— as far between as the maiden and the crone. Entire histories between the two clips.

Bernadine.

I'm not sure you got what you deserved, but none of us ever do, do we?

In dreams.

The Promoter

They were stacking life-sized cardboard cutouts of Jesus in the alley. They were clearing out the joint. I admired the energy of the working men.

"We're on a schedule, boys!"

The Theater was dark.

It was an in between time. Here in Queens.

I could not find the script and the Director was AWOL. Last seen in a Murder Joint in the Five Points. I was getting nervous. Not clear on who was in charge. Who to trust in the days of the White Slave Trade.

All the chorus girls were Regional Champions of Dance Marathons. Piranhas in silk. Razor-blade lipstick and perfume. The leading men all had comb overs and smelled of morning afters, mornings following nightmares, nightmares of teeth turned to cake and impotence.

The show must go on.

The place reeked of gaslight and garlic. The costumes were rough and ill-fitting. They were throwing dead rabbits on the stage to send messages. They were passing out hypos in the lobby. They were huffing vapors on the street and sniffing glue.

We turned the lights up and sent out the ghost of Spiro Agnew. Test the waters. See what the savages would do. They howled and raised their fists.

"Good night for red meat," we said.

We sent out the Minstrel Singers and Comic Negroes. We sent out the Italian Act and the Yiddishers. Good audience, tonight. If we're lucky it's a bottle before midnight and maybe a comfort call to the Girl Singer who's Anybody's Baby for a hotel dinner. Delmonico's and oysters. You should hear her sing when she got the red light on.

The Sentimental Irisher was sick and with no one to sing of old Galway Bay, I had to go on. I used the cardboard cut outs of Jesus. That's all I remember. And I did a few choice and tasty steps. Doing my best Ronald Reagan. A jig to amuse the people. But mostly I opened myself to the audience. In the great and dark Theater.

On the night before the Apocalypse, the Cinema-Photographer was valiant. He captured every hostile light and beat back the dawn. The Best Boy hung on. The First Grip ascended. The AWOL Director called "Scene," after Newt Gingrich did his thing. And the Theater was empty.

I stood there on that stage. In broken continuity. This is what I mean to tell you. Without logical progression. I stood on that stage alone. In the broken history light of my times. After Karl Rove did his whole white face routine. I just stood there. And opened myself to the audience.

And it was a hell of a thing I saw. Not what I expected at all. Standing there alone on stage.

Faces that knew how the trick was done before you did it. And still stayed for the trick. Faces that knew more about the Theater than you ever did standing on the boards. And were still hungry for stories.

Faces. Just watching. Looking for some sign of home.

We ended the show with some high-concept Grand Guignol. And played the National Anthem. Give the people what they want.

After the show, people went home like virgins. Like old maids. Just like coming home after Monsignor's show in Manhattan with ethnic skits and patriotic songs from a long lost home.

The show must go on.

Aquarium World

I was in this aquarium world where the words you say come out of your mouth and swim in the environment like schools of fish.

There was a grammar in this aquarium world that was identical to choreography. Communication was in the movement. Words became bodies and they danced with other bodies and accomplished entire paragraphs. The elegance of fish. The punctuation was top shelf.

Some of the dances were transcendent. And in this aquarium world what that meant. Transcendent. Was that the bodies moved in ways that opened locks which opened doors and cleared out clogged pipes. It was all about liquidity in the aquarium world. Cash flow. Oil flow. Water flow. Blood flow.

So the living waters of life could flow.

Like some Big Muddy. Major artery. Corpus Christi. Some Hudson River. Some Missouri River. Let it flow! We're talking American Engineering here. Army Corp of Engineers. Like some irrigation system hardwired into reality. Branches on the vine. In some exceptional America. Some Shining City on a Hill. This is the way it was in the aquarium world I was in.

And it was kind of like drowning by thirst. In this aquarium world. I gotta tell you. I was underwater in the aquarium world and dying of thirst. I mean.

Broke my heart. Swimming back and forth behind

the glass. Back and forth behind the glass. Looking for a long-tall, cool, drink of water.

And when I woke up from the aquarium world I could feel the rhythm in my veins. Pumping. Pumping. Pushing life through the pipelines of my body. The Great Alaska Pipeline of the body. Drill, baby! Drill!

I was thirsty as hell. Drank big old plastic glasses of bathroom water. After I woke up from the aquarium world. Like a man come in from the desert. Some desert rat coming up for sweet tea.

Just like Jonah. All sunburnt, whale-swallowed and whatnot.

Thirsty.

As my words swam across the horizon.

Me and Lindy

I was sleeping and me and Lindy—Lucky Lindy—were making our way to France. And it was pretty special. A nation addicted to motion. Stood still and watched. We're talking technology here, children. They got cables and telegraphs and telephones and wires. In one big Right Now. A jaded nation stood still and watched. As me and Lindy made our way to France. Like they were watching a moon walk or something.

We went to some suburban party. A gathering of the tribe. In the suburbs. When they walked on the moon. A circling of the wagons.

Anyway, me and Lindy were on our way to France. In this dream. And Babe Ruth was just whacking the shit out of that thing and Hollywood was providing us with even more efficient household gods. You should have seen the line of women waiting to catch a glimpse of Rudolph Valentino in his casket. Half-hoping. Half-dreading. His Magic Sheik would once more rise to its Saharan glory. Right there on 49th St.

Al Capone was doing his thing, too. Which was always a kind of family joke. We lived in Chicagoland in the seventies. Grandma and Pappy back in Idaho always seemed titillated and worried. Dad said they seemed to think that old Scar-face was still massacring St. Valentine. Rat-a-tat-tat. Just like "Gangbusters" and the "Untouchables".

"Who knows what evil lurks in the hearts of men? The Shadow knows."

So anyway. Me and Lindy. Approaching France. And I got the notion that there really ought to be more. I mean. This is in the dream. And I'm thinking. This is how we can really mark this moment. Make a splash.

Say Hallelujah! Praise the Lord!

So I decide to climb out on the wing and perform some complicated maneuver. Dare Devil stuff. And I'm kind of swashbuckling. I mean. I'm all Douglas Fairbanks with that shit.

And I'm walking out on the wing. Me and Lindy approaching France. And God. He's sitting on my shoulder. In my dream. And God. He says:

"Awesome dude."

And I say, "Fucking A, man!"

We share a grinning thumbs-up.

And he says. This is God talking. Sitting on my shoulder. He says:

"Who's flying the plane?"

Double Vision

The Krishnas were out of control. They dressed in clown costumes with big red noses and prop-paint cans that said ISKCON on the side. They were making a lot of noise.

Hinduism was like some flooding river.

I saw Pure Land Buddhists carrying placards. I saw wealthy young ladies with boyish flapper bodies in love with Krishnamurti.

The storefront Bishops and 125th St. Music Store Prophets were selling Casio keyboards. They had mimeographs and high smelling dittos full of testimonies and witnesses.

There was this guy in front of the Wurlitzer store in the mall. He was playing "The Entertainer" real slow.

The Jews were wearing hats and cracking wise.

The Muslims were weaving obligatory/ecstatic patterns which kind of riled up the Irish rug makers. There were controversies and questions of authorship concerning labyrinths.

I was dressed in my baptismal robes. I was washed whiter than snow.

I asked them to quiet down. I stood at the mike and tried to call them to order.

Joseph Smith was right there in front too, challenging any one who would come to two falls out of three. The Zoroasterians did the wave. A marvel of mass coordination. And out there somewhere behind the bleachers a couple of Carthusians refused to shout.

I tapped the mike. I read the public service announcements about the brown acid. And reminded people to hydrate frequently.

All that was going on.

But time stopped and split. And a whole other movie started to play on a different screen.

I can't tell you what I saw on the other screen. It would mean erasing everything that was on the first screen—the screen with the mike and the veiled Jains and Rastafarians and African Exorcists and old ladies who attend lectures at the Ethical Culture Society.

And you can't see what I saw without the first screen. The screen with the Methodists and Thug-gees and hash-crazed Assassins and twirlers of Mother Ann Lee. You gotta have both screens if you're going to see.

Aw, what the hell. That lady from Jefferson Airplane up there on the stage, she just keeps yelling about "morning maniac music." And the silence coming from beyond is intoxicating. It speaks like a lover gasping.

I'll keep my eye on both screens. And trust that I am watched.

Invisible Jesus

I was at the Second Avenue Deli before it moved to Thirty-Third and Third, eating a corned beef sandwich with brown mustard on rye and a root beer. (You gotta take half the meat off to eat it.)

A waitress with shaved eyebrows and a wig asked me how I liked my sandwich. I adjusted my toupee, stroked my Van Dyke, and swallowed.

"Fine," I said.

"Glad you're enjoying it," she said.

"You and me both, sister," I said.

She pulled up her bra strap and gave me a wink.

I winked back at her.

We were on the same side of the fence.

"Hey babe," I said, "when you get off?"

"Who wants to know?" she says.

"Me, myself, and I," I say.

"You don't say?" she said.

This was getting us nowhere.

"You going my way, babe?" I asked.

"I guess I got to take the next train, soldier," she said.

"That's the way the cards fall, doll."

"You said it, mister."

"You're alright, sister."

"You're okay, mister."

Corned beef on rye. Man, it just melts in your mouth. Eat a pickle. I'm just saying. It's good.

I was riding with the invisible Jesus. Riding with the King. And boys. Let me tell you. We were bad.

Communiqué # 91863

Nothing to report tonight. Or at least next to nothing. All the technical boys and girls went home. Nobody here to dress the actors or set the stage. It's just us. Beneath the lights. On the boards.

And we are losing the signal. Late night radio. We're almost out of bounds. Beyond the reach of the great transmitters. On the edge of town. There are reports of fires. On the outskirts.

It's all static and signal. It's all about turning each and every way. Like a Heliotrope. And standing by the

TV in certain positions because the antenna can't. You move your arm into position. With a certain touch. And signal comes clear.

We're in the borderlands, boys. We're in Twilight.

And a voice comes over the air.

"Can you hear me Radio Free Europe? Come in, Radio Free Europe. This is Jesse James."

"Copy that, Jesse James, we read you and we clear you. Go ahead Jesse James."

And a voice comes over the air.

"Radio Free Europe. This is Jesse James. Communiqué Number 91863. Ready to commence."

"This is Radio Free Europe. Go ahead. Jesse James."

"When it comes to these things it's a matter of, 'you frame the question, you own the answer.'"

"This is Radio Free Europe to Jesse James. Does this complete your message?"

"This is Jesse James to Radio Free Europe. Yes. Yes, this completes our message."

"When it comes to these things it's a matter of, 'you frame the question, you own the answer.'"

"Over and out."

"Yes, this is Jesse James saying, 'over and out.'"

Then we lost the signal.

The Portrait

The king commissioned a new state portrait of himself. And the Madison Avenue boys came up with a humdinger. It was a mirror. Everybody saw what they wanted to see. And I shit you not. It was a slam dunk.

It was all high fives and you-da-mans.

Like we'd made the cover of the Rolling Stone. Time Magazine's Person of the Year.

Anyways. I was chewing my Juicy Fruit—and let me tell you boys, this was when I was still dating the Doublemint Twins—and I started looking at the new official state portrait.

I was just chewing my gum and looking at the portrait of the king.

Damned if I didn't disapprove of what I saw.

Bubblegum all over my face and ugliness in my heart.

It was then that I knew that the king must die.

Roots

In this one I was pumping water at the well. Priming the pump. And then waiting until the water ran clear. Pump. Pump. Pump.

And it wouldn't come clear.

And I couldn't find a connection between the Americans before World War II and the Americans after. Much seemed to depend upon this connection. In the dream. Entire family histories and contests between fathers and sons. Mothers and daughters. Cain and Abel. Ronald Reagan. Lives in the balance. The victors write history.

I was pumping and my arm was getting tired. Waiting for the water to come clear.

I got bits of clotted Steinbeck and great hunks of John Dos Passos ripped from midsections. The water was running rusty.

There were chunks of Mark Twain that looked like

gefelte fish in a jar and Jay Gatsby strolling across Long Island lawns.

America came in a parade. A succession of floats and Cadillacs. She was proud and matronly. She danced low down and moaned the Georgia Crawl. She marched for Suffrage and tended the hearth fires. I saw Carrie Nation and Michelle Bachman. I saw Mata Hari and Little Sheba in the Columbian Exposition in Chicago in 1893.

Then came Wild Bill Hickock and Doc Holiday. And Pretty Boy Floyd and this guy who killed two people holding up an Edward Hopper gas station in Utah in the mid-seventies.

I saw the Oddfellows and the Rotarians. I saw the Eagles and the Shriners. I saw the Ku Klux Klan and the Daughters of the American Revolution. I saw business men on Main Street in Short Sleeved Shirts. I saw the Knights of Columbus and the Masons. I saw the Good Citizens.

And then great big chunks of Cyndi Lauper videos and Johnny Thunders and the New York Dolls having a Personality Crisis. And the Moral Majority. And Operation Rescue. And credit cards.

I saw Romper Room and Tom Terrific. I saw the Fabulous Furry Freak Brothers and my Straight Arrow Dad panicking in Ann Arbor during Hash Bash in 1980.

I saw the Hula Hoop and the Frisbee. I saw Action Figures and Market Segments. I saw purchasing power and Pokemon. I saw Rock and Roll and the Twist. I saw for myself that there ain't no cure for the summer time blues.

I saw George Wallace and Fred Hampton. The Symbionese Liberation Army. I saw the Lesbian Collective march down Main Street in Seneca Falls dressed in topless womb costumes in 1989. (They were installed in a permanent protest against nuclear weapons just outside the Army Depot, where they kept the missiles, and the frogs turned white and deer were born with five legs—and were surprised when the locals focused on their topless lesbian marches more than the fact that frogs were turning white and deer were being born with five legs and their children were drinking the water.)

My arm was getting tired.

I couldn't find the connection. The volume had been turned up. Rush Limbaugh was getting loud. In the 90's.

I saw pictures of my ancestors. Old photographs. Guys in overalls and women haunted by childbirth. Gaunt. Fierce. Avaricious as the sea.

We don't look like them. We aren't that hungry.

It woke me up. The water ran clear. Like one more escape from Eden. I woke up laughing. Laughing until it hurt. Really enjoying it too. Just a really good dream. Like a bloody cut under cold water and direct pressure. Running clear.

They tore up the roots. There is no connection.

We're on our own, children.

Time to dream ourselves up a new America.

Communique #91863: The Eyes in the Night
They were parading down Fifth Avenue with the

head of Antonin Artaud on a stick. It wasn't even a mob. It was just rush hour traffic.

And for its part, the head of Antonin Artaud, to tell you the truth, it seemed to be having the time of it's life. Riding the waves of progress. Mugging for the crowd. Making faces.

Like for once. Everything was in sync. The Unia Mystica.

And I was watching it like on TV. There was distance. If you know what I mean.

Funniest thing I've ever seen.

And on another channel they were building a bonfire of the vanities. There were giraffes. And there were endless video loops caught live on cell phones, of young men and women, naked and beautiful, leaping from platforms into the flames—swan dives—fat crackling in the night like microwavable pork rinds— each landing greeted with roars and cheers and high fives—like the Yankees had won the pennant and ladies and gentlemen, the Bronx is burning. And then shots of the trucks bringing in the logs to fuel the fire. And the sound of Howard Cosell's voice.

I saw rows and rows of white men in suits. They were taking a seminar. I got my hands on the brochure, but it got snapped away in the wind from the great fans set up for the glamor shot. I couldn't really get the gist. But it involved advanced techniques in swallowing loathsome things. Toads and okra. The rows and rows of white men in suits. They learned to suppress their gag reflexes. They ate tarantulas and scorpions. They ate slugs and leeches. But there was a sidebar with a video that revealed the progress of the cancer through-out the entire seminar. And everyone was afraid of getting kicked off the island.

I think that was on Yahoo.

Then on another network they were having a Minority Marathon. Nonstop close ups of faces of minority citizens. No emotion at all whatsoever. Naked eyes. Face after face after face.

These faces were punctuated with faces of white people in Detroit. White people in Manhattan. White people in Central Pennsylvania. I caught my own image in a reflection from the flat screen.

A quick shot of a young woman peeling an artichoke.

Corks were floating in a pool. I saw yellow balloons released after having been submerged under water. We were all caught in the turmoil. Everybody was a little rubbery. Like when they film in HD and you've only got a regular TV.

There were people who were grotesque in their stained underpants, gesticulating wildly. There were scenes of steroid rage. Cathartic beatings of perceived enemies. A permanent revival. In a cartoon America.

I saw myself waving a floppy Bible. Just like Jimmy Swaggart. I saw myself just really nailing that sermon and leaving the folks in a state. Fired up. Ready to go.

So I pulled the plug.

But the after-image remained.

I pulled the plug. And I saw a face. I've just seen a face I can't recall the time or place. Just looking.

Just looking at me like Mr. Rousseau's lion.

Jacob

A number of years earlier I'd screwed my brother over. It was pretty easy, really. He was all reaction and all about the right now. My brother. He sold me his birthright for some lentil stew. I'm just saying.

Anyway. I'd made my rounds and come to my margins and called in all my chips and.

OK, let's be up front, I had nowhere else to go. So I decided to go home.

I left a message for my brother. Told him I was coming home. After I'd screwed him over and was now sort of down on my luck. Real prodigal son stuff.

Next thing I know, he leaves a message for me. Seems he's gonna meet me at the airport. Seems he's got a message to deliver in person.

So I freaked, right? I mean you don't know my brother. He was never the sharpest blade in the drawer, and he didn't have a neck. All chest and muscle and testosterone. This kid had pubic hair when he was seven. If you know what I mean.

I was feeling pretty guilty about what I did to him. But even more so. I was worried about what he would do. After I had done what I had done to him. I was quick on my feet and able to dance. But this time there wasn't a lot of room.

So anyway. The night before my flight home. Holed up with a six pack in a Red Roof Inn by the airport. I had a dream.

This guy came and gave me the look. In the dream. You know what I'm talking about. He gave me the look.

And I couldn't just let him get away with that. So I gave him the look back.

And then he said, "You want a piece of me?"

And I said, "You talking to me?"

And then we sort of stood around and avoided each other's eyes.

Anyway. Long story short. We started scuffling. Mostly because we couldn't find a way out. It was half-hearted, I'm telling you.

And then it wasn't. A nose got bloodied. And then it was go time.

He was beating the shit out of me, but I couldn't let go. He was huge and fit. His fists were like sledgehammers. I got my licks in too. That was pretty clear. I think I dislocated his hip. Or maybe he dislocated mine.

Anyway. It was totally out of control.

In my dream.

We rioted all night long. And the sun was starting to rise. And I had nothing left but meanness.

Boys. Let me tell you, I was in pretty bad shape. But I wouldn't yield. I wouldn't throw in the towel. What was he supposed to do? I just clung to him. With everything I had. Like some sort of wolverine. And the sun was coming up.

And he said, "I gotta go, this dream is about to end."

And I said sort of nonsensically, "I know you are, but what am I?"

He said, "No really, I'm serious. You're going to wake up any time now. And I can't be here."

"I won't ever let you go. I will cling to you like a leech. Until I suck you dry. Don't underestimate me. I know where you live."

I was talking smack. I was talking all crazy. I was telling the truth.

"OK, OK," he said. "You win. I love you."

"I love you too," I said.

And when I woke up at the airport. My brother was there. He took my carry-on. He drove me home.

"What you been up to?" he asked while traffic was backed up on the Jersey side trying to get through the tunnel.

"I wrestled with an angel with a dirty face and saw God."

"Far out," he said, "I hope you're hungry. I made lentils."

The Tug of the River

It was remarkable. After the starburst. After the explosion. The dust settled.

Let's be clear here. In this dream. It was not the explosion that was of interest. It was the settling. The settling of the dust.

And the pregnant stillness.

I was reading Mark Twain. "Life on the Mississippi". I was reading about how all the pilots had to memorize the river. All those riverboat pilots. The river that always changed. About how the pilots had to remember that what had once been a clear channel was now and could be next year a sandbar. Or maybe a clear channel again.

Or risk running aground.

I was reading a book about the building of the

Brooklyn Bridge. And an America I couldn't feel any-more.

I was looking at my father. Carrying an entire na-tion on his back. It seemed to be made of sticks. With-out mud. The nation on his back. Light penetrating every crevice. Ingeniously woven. For easy transport. And he was slogging uphill. With his rickety structure on his back. My father.

I mean I was just watching that. Sisyphus.

And feeling the current. Feeling the rhythm. Hear-ing the call of the river. The call of the canal. The rhythm of transport. Got my foot a tapping. Hand me down my walking cane.

I fantasized about letting loose. Setting the woods on fire. I imagined lawlessness and orgies.

I made my peace with stones.

The dream was over. I didn't even wake up. It was just over. And I was still dreaming. But in this one I could smell the river. And recognize the old longing.

Like a virgin. I pondered these things and treasured them in my heart.

Like a man. Almost old and used and worn out.

I felt the pulse of the land. The tug of the river.

Be True To Your School (After Brian Wilson)

I was in Paris waiting in the receiving line to shake hands with Benjamin Franklin. I was next in line.

And wouldn't you know it. Suddenly the Baal Shem Tov was there. He started singing and clapping his hands. Dancing around like an idiot. I was mortified.

And then before I knew it, St. Francis of Assisi

was there too. And he started singing as well. Clapping along with the Besht, and even providing counter rhythms and interesting percussionary variations. Getting his groove on. It was disgusting.

And before I knew it Krishna was leading a bunch of Gopi Girls in some really sweet close harmonies. The cast of Hair started singing "The Age of Aquarius". And Shirley Caesar started stalking the stage doing a sweet version of "Satisfied Mind", which figured perfectly as a a kind of counter-melody.

And Little Richard was there too. And Marvin Gaye. And Chuck Berry. And Jerry Lee Lewis. And Jimmie Rodgers. And comically, Donovan. (He was a hoot. In his English feathers and kaftans.)

I can't tell you how deeply ashamed I was. Like I was a rube.

It came my turn to shake the hand of Benjamin Franklin. Make my impression as an up and comer. A real go-getter and booster of Liberty.

And I couldn't help myself. I did the Georgia Crawl. I did the Watusi. I just lost it with the Qawwali singers. Like a native son of the land of a thousand dances. I like it like that. My face burning with shame. Like I was vomiting. Like I couldn't help myself.

And then my turn came. And Benjamin Franklin shook my hand.

And didn't even notice the choir that had come with me. Didn't seem to hear the songs or the chants or the drums.

It was then that the Besht. Baal Shem Tov. Leaned over to me. And said. This is what he said:

"Let us do our living right down here."

And he pointed to the Rev. Gary Davis. And gave a shout out.

Suddenly, Benjamin Franklin turned to me. I mean he was already shaking the hand of the guy in line after me. Benjamin Franklin was wearing a tux. It was then that Benjamin Franklin turned to me and whispered:

"Viva la revolucion!"

A Real Good Yegg

There was a guy in the alley. He had clearly been around the block a few times. A real good yegg.

"Any thing I can do for you, pal?" I said.

"Gotta coffin nail?" he said.

"Do I? And how? I got Kents."

"Kents? With the exclusive Micronite filter?"

"You said a mouthful, mister."

"You can take it to the bank, son."

I gave him a light and looked at his face. This boy was a thousand miles from home. Sometimes you get so far, you can't never come back.

"Mind if I ask you a question, pilgrim?" I asked, lighting a cigarette of my own.

"It's a free country, ain't it?"

"This citizen says 'yeah.'"

"Don't kid yourself, that's the goods."

"How does it feel? How does it feel to be too far to come back?"

"Well, let me tell you, brother. It feels alright. Until it doesn't."

Up In the Attic

I was cleaning out the attic in the haunted house. We were going to move. I was half-choked by the dust and animal dung.

The past in the attic of the haunted house lived in boxes that had been opened and disturbed like asbestos-wrapped steam pipes. That's what happens when the present goes on too long. You loot the past.

I was sorting through the keepsakes of more than one generation that was going to fade away. I was feeling ruthless. But the particularity of moments kept announcing itself in the randomness of the keepsakes.

I found an Amtrak ticket stub from New York to Albany stashed in a self-help book all about how you always marry your mother or your father.

I found cocktail napkins from the early seventies with bawdy cartoons. I found whole treasure troves of S and H Green Stamp books just waiting to be redeemed.

I found 45 rpm singles. "The Shady Lady of Shady Lane". Carl Perkins singing "Blue Suede Shoes".

I found Tonka Trucks and Hotwheels. I found mint condition copies of both "The Sensuous Man" and "The Sensuous Woman".

I found a ticket stub from a Who concert in Detroit after all those kids had been trampled in Cincinnati. I found My Dad's Harry Belafonte album on which Bob Dylan played harmonica. I found a dried rose petal that had fallen from heaven when some folks saw a vision of the Virgin Mary in Flushing, Queens.

I found the blackjack my Great-grandfather used when he was Chief of Police in Talapoosa, Georgia and took no shit from hard-boiled sharecroppers and uppity nigras. He was a bad man. Like Stack-a-lee.

I found GI Joes with life-like hair and a Kung-Fu Grip. I found a postcard from a girl who really seemed to miss me. And a leather peace sign on a leather thong.

I found the Derby hat that I had impossibly found in the closet of my father's childhood bedroom in Grangeville, Idaho—the very hat that upon discovering, I had immediately donned and then, as if possessed, inexplicably and expertly channeled the comic Chaplin-walk up and down the bedroom, to the amazement of my loving grandparents.

Man, I miss that hat.

I found county fair prizes and milk crates. I found ancient plastic squeeze bottles of Mennen Antiperspirant. I found photographs from my parent's honeymoon in Salt Lake City.

I found photos of me in a "Cub Power" T-shirt. And my sister in that pixie cut when old guys would come up to her and deliberately pretend that she was a boy.

I found Nat King Cole albums. I found Ann Arbor Art work. Menstrual Prints. They just sat down on paper, bled, and called it Art.

I found postcards of Tristan Tzara and the young homo-erotic Elvis. Jimmy Dean and Jack Kerouac.

I found evidence of the presence of Santa Teresa and a Crucifix blessed by JP II. There were apocalyptic tracts and empty condom boxes. There were books about Bonnie and Clyde. And a skate key.

It was all up in the attic. And the house was haunted. I kept hearing snatches of Gershwin tunes.

EPILOGUE

Lunch with the Rabbi

I was having lunch with Isaac Luria. And we were talking origins. And practical problems like how you find the skin and bone to control the divine influx, because, God knows, if it's too soft the damn thing flails around like an unmanned fire hose.

The guy who built the Brooklyn Bridge. Washington Roebling. Suspension bridge across the East River. Son of a great man. He believed the key was to make it stiff. Rigid.

I excused myself from the table.

The advertisements in the men's room were all from the same outfit. It was like being in a subway car. I could feel the ancient railroad sway. Everything smelled like Amtrak.

I went back to the table. The Rabbi wiped his mouth with a linen napkin.

"You never get used to passing between worlds," he said. "Last night I brought flowers home to my wife and she burst into flames. I almost drowned on the marble steps of the foyer of an apartment building I've never visited. I have an ulcer."

I thought about pretending I hadn't heard him. I thought about maybe just insisting upon another take. I thought about the sheer utility of denial.

"Silly Rabbi," I said, "Kicks are for trids."

"You do know," Isaac Luria said, "it's still going to be here when you wake up, right?"

I stood up then. Got out of my finely upholstered seat. And I said. This is what I said to the Rabbi:

"Yeah."

And he said. This is what he said back to me:

"It just never was ever going to be any different."

And I said.

This is what I said:

"Amen."

Jack and Me

I was stone blind drunk with Jack London. Me and Jack. On a tear. And his teeth were all rotten. And his friends were all vultures. And he just didn't give a damn.

You can only pretend to be someone for so long. Sooner or later you're going to have to become someone. Someone invisible. Like for real and not in some story you write.

Jack had gone just about as far as you can go.

We were sitting on a dirty beach in Santa Cruz. It was night time and we'd built a beach fire of driftwood. All the street kids hovered around. Dancing with fire-shadows. Erased in stolen prescription drugs and earnest handshakes. They danced like flames licking logs. On a dirty beach in Santa Cruz.

I was seeing double. I was holding off the spins. Me and Jack on a tear. And he was wrestling with a stranger on the beach. He just wouldn't let go. It was like everything depended upon him not letting go. Veins were bulging. Joints were being ripped out of sockets. The two of them out there on the beach. Beating the crap out of one another. They were dancing on my last nerve.

I stood up. I started singing John Denver songs at the top of my lungs. I worshiped at a different church. I cut ole Jack loose.

I just had to get off that dirty beach.

When I finally reached the boardwalk, Jack was there waiting for me.

"Do you see what I'm saying now?" he asked.

I threw up all over his canvas boat shoes.

"I guess," I said, gasping for breath.

There was a sob in my throat. Like the gurgle of water down a drain. I just stood there and watched as Jack and I disappeared. Became invisible.

"I guess," I said.

And disappeared just like a cut diamond in water.

Traitors

In this one I was standing on the tip of the island looking out onto New York Harbor. I was waving goodbye to a ship that was sending Big Bill Haywood off to Soviet Russia.

Some kind of forced exile. Or escape. I misremember which.

I had reliable intelligence from the future which led me to believe that the old Wobbly would not fare well in the Soviet Union. He would die bitter and alone, longing for the long lonesome nights of the prairie. And the wells of whiskey and women. Pumping continuously into the hard-eyed mouths. Of fresh-faced boys. Beyond the sight of their mothers. In mining camps.

It was the innocence he mourned. And the photographic-flash of mattering. The sheer joy of creating yourself and no one being able to stop you from doing it.

Big Bill Haywood was about to become invisible.

So anyway, in this one I was waving goodbye to a ship that was sending Big Bill Haywood off to Soviet Russia. And me and Robert Ford—that dirty little coward—were passing a bottle back and forth.

"Son of a bitch was a terrorist, you know?" I said, taking a snort.

"Yeah, I know." Robert took a slug of the bottle.

"Got what he deserved, if you ask me," I said.

He took the bottle back and looked at me.

"You ever get what you deserved, Pilgrim?" he asked.

"I guess not," I said, looking at the ground.

"Me neither," he said and spit.

I took a slug of the bottle, snuck another peek at him and decided there wasn't any meat on those bones.

Big Bill Haywood steamed out into the horizon. A reliable source from the future had it that he died bitter and drunk in some sad room.

Me and Robert Ford watched as the story played itself out. Passing that bottle back and forth. Just passing it back and forth, the ship with its smoke plume getting smaller and the dream growing larger with every instant of its betrayal.

And a whole continent beckoned when we turned our backs.

DOWN THE PLYMOUTH ROAD

"Jesus said, 'Become passers-by.'"
The Gospel of Thomas

1

I was walking down the Plymouth Road with the Rabbi and he was showing me stuff.

He showed me this homeless guy who lived at the 79th St. Boat Basin. He'd been a boxer. He was a loser. He died of exposure one cold night.

He showed me this old lady living in a luxury apartment on Grand Ave. in Queens. Her husband died. And then her brother died. And then she started to sell her possessions and her fancy clothes. And they evicted her and she went into the shelter system and was just swallowed.

He showed me this woman who had a cyst on her ovary and told this guy she knew that she was going to die and tried to get the guy to adopt her son. And the cyst was benign and she'd been trying to pawn the kid off on anyone she could find. She was done being a mother. The kid set the apartment on fire and died in the fire.

I was walking with the Rabbi and he was showing me stuff.

"Why you got to show me this stuff?" I asked.

He lifted his arm, and with the rustling of the cape, I caught a whiff of a city-run old folks home.

"We're chasing daylight here," he said, "we don't have a lot of time."

"No, seriously. Why do I have to see all this stuff? What about the other stuff?"

"The other stuff? Son, you don't know what you're asking."

"Oh come off it!"

He lifted his other arm, and with the rustling of the cape, I caught a glimpse of the hyena and the gazelle.

"Son, you're not ready."

"But...."

He lifted his eyes and what I saw in the twinkling of an eye....

I was not ready.

•

I was walking to Plymouth and I met the Rabbi on the road. He was laughing.

"What are you laughing about?" I asked.

"Check this out," he said and then held up an iPad. "It's a slide show of all your former selves."

I took a look and winced.

"C'mon, you were so cute!"

"You're sick, you know that?," but I was kind of laughing myself.

I lingered over one of the former selves.

"What was I thinking?"

"I know, right?"

"Well," I asked, "are we going to do this thing?"

"Might as well get started."

He pulled out the straight razor and removed my skin. I stood there without my skin.

"It's still not deep enough, is it?" I asked.

"No, it's not."

"Rabbi, can I have my eyebrows back? The sun is so bright and I need to squint."

He gave me my eyebrows back. I squinted. I felt the wind on my muscles, so raw now without skin.

I walked down the Plymouth Road.

•

I was walking down the Plymouth Road and I came upon the devil. He broke my jaw. Just hauled off and busted me in the chops.

"What you want to go and do a thing like that for?" I asked, all blood and outrage.

"You got a big mouth, pilgrim," he said. "I hear you been talking."

"I didn't give nothing away," I pleaded.

He broke my nose.

"Listen bitch, I decide what it means to give something away! You got that?"

"I didn't say nothing! You didn't have to go and do that!"

"You make me sick," he said. "You couldn't keep a secret if your life depended upon it. You're weak. You're a joke. You're NOTHING!"

"And....scene."

We both cracked up.

"Jeeze, you didn't have to really break my nose," I

cried.

"What about you? 'I must pay the rent! I can't pay the rent!' You're such a diva!"

We sort of collapsed together in hilarity, me and the devil.

After awhile it kind of hurts your stomach to keep laughing.

"You do know that you can break every bone in my body, and I will still find my way home, right?"

"Yeah, I know."

"Then why do you keep ambushing me on the road?"

"It ain't personal kid, it's just business."

"Anyway, I just want you to know I don't hold a grudge."

"Well, that's just fine."

"That's the way the cookie crumbles."

"You're alright, pilgrim."

"You're not so bad yourself."

I stuck him with my knife like a pig.

•

They got a room where they keep all the sorrow. It looks a lot like a salt barn in the northeast. In any case, it's very easy to get a pass to enter that room. To enter the room of sorrow.

They got another room where they keep all the ecstasy. It looks a lot like a salt barn in the northeast. And you can wait your whole life and never get a pass to enter the room of ecstasy.

You go down the road long enough and you realize that it's the same room. The room where they keep all the sorrow and the room where they keep all the ecstasy. It looks a lot like a salt barn in the northeast.

I've been down the road long enough and I don't really know what to make of that. It's the same room. It's the same frigging room.

It was either the Rabbi or the devil who told me once that I was the salt of the earth. Truth be told, sometimes they sound a lot like one another. And if you really want to know the truth, sometimes I have a hard time telling them apart.

None of that really matters though. They give you a pass to enter the room when you're born. It looks a lot like a salt barn in the northeast.

What you do with the pass is up to you.

•

I was further on down the road and I met the Rabbi. He was waiting for me and said, "I got something you need to see." And he showed me his iPad and there was just nothing on that screen.

"I know what you did," he said.

"I don't even know how to begin to feel guilty," I said.

"I'm not asking you to feel guilty."

"Then what's your point?"

"Once there was a seed," he said, "and it grew large and became a tree and many birds made their homes in its branches."

"And that tree killed the lawn and was a bit of an eyesore in the neighborhood. What's your point?"

"Yeah, but the birds....they had a place to build their nests."

"So what? The world is full of opportunists."

"Don't give me that, you know what it means to have others depend on you."

"Once I dreamed that all the trees walked about when we were asleep. It was a lie, wasn't it?"

"I'm afraid so, pilgrim."

"Still, it hurts to set roots...."

"....because they will always be pulled up."

"Yep."

"And birds will always need somewhere to nest," he said.

"Rabbi?"

"Yes?"

"The birds... You sent them, didn't you?"

"I sent the birds."

"Rabbi?"

"Yes?"

"Thank you."

"You're welcome. Now hand over that knife, there's been enough killing for the day."

I was walking down the Plymouth road, my feet like roots newly ripped from fertile soil, flinging dirt across the road.

•

They got the whole deal set up on the Plymouth Road. It's like a spiritual toll system. You want to get from point A to point B? You got to pay the man.

At regular intervals you encounter fearsome angels with fiery swords. If you do not have the secret password—the secret name of the angel—why, that angel is just going to cut you down. You will drown on the steps of marble, you will emerge from the orchard a broken man. And worst of all you will not make your connecting flight.

Because, after all, it is all about getting home for the holidays.

In any case, on the Plymouth Road, everywhere you look they got fiery chariots ascending and descending. They got prophets on their way up and they got prophets on their way down. Ascending and descending in fiery chariots. This is all on the Plymouth Road, you understand.

And sometimes the way forward flows from the cracked lips of the prophet on his way up and other times it flows from the bleeding lips of the prophet who is on his way down. Either way, you've got to maintain your sea legs when the way forward flows.

Yes, indeedy! They got it all worked out on the Plymouth Road. It's where the weight of your life finds the foundation to hold it! Woo doggie!

Listen up, folks! They're going to try and tell you that you're doomed. I mean, on the Plymouth Road. All the demons snapping at your heels. All those demons—they are just forever waiting to tell you that you are doomed. But they're wrong.

You're not doomed. You're just not home yet—gotta ways to go yet, that's all—on the Plymouth Road.

Might as well splurge on a brand new pair of shoes when you know you're going to need them. Know what I mean?

●

I was walking down the Plymouth Road and the Rabbi was walking too.

"I guess we're pretty much stuck with one another," I said.

"I guess," he replied.

"Rabbi?"

"Yes?"

And then after awhile I said, "Never mind."

We just walked down the Plymouth Road.

2

I was walking down the Plymouth Road, it was just me and the Rabbi, and then we came upon Jesus. He was hiding ridiculously behind a potted plant. Invisible in plain sight like a purloined letter. We waved at him and called his name, but he just ignored us.

"You know we can see you," I said.

I turned to the Rabbi, but he was no where to be found.

"You're not fooling anyone behind that potted plant," I said. "In fact, the whole thing is really kind of infantile. We can see you. I'm just saying."

"Maybe he doesn't want to be seen," the Rabbi said, "maybe you should just ignore him."

I turned to say something but the Rabbi was no-where to be found. Jesus peered out from behind the potted plant.

"But I can see you!" I shouted.

"There's no need to get worked up about it," the Rabbi said.

I was starting to get angry. This was just stupid.

"I mean... you're right there!"

"You really need to learn to let it go, pilgrim."

We just kept walking, me and the Rabbi.

"It just chaps my ass...."

"I'm just saying... let it go."

"He was right *there*."

•

I got a castle in my soul and you can't enter into this castle unless you take off your shoes. God lives in the castle in my soul—but when God enters even the Father, Son and Holy Ghost wait outside. (This is true up to the point at which it becomes a lie. It's not like I'm some kind of Unitarian, or something.)

I got a castle in my soul and it only becomes manifest when I build it. My ancestors used to sing a song: "Working on a building, a Holy Ghost building!"

This is what they were talking about. There is always something else that we are doing whenever we do what we are doing. I suspect that what the ancestors referred to as "Wisdom" was the ability to see double.

There is a castle in my soul, and the bride and the bridegroom, they enter therein. They close the doors, they draw up the bridge. What goes on between them in the castle in my soul is not for my eyes. But I'd be a fool not to join the party outside the castle walls. I'd be a fool not to dance to such music.

There is a castle in my soul. I've spent half my life besieging it and the other half trying to tear it down from within. It just always stands. It doesn't feel my assaults. It just always stands.

I got a castle in my soul, and the banners that fly from its spires and minarets are spectacular. They just really are something else.

•

I was walking down the Plymouth Road and the Rabbi turned to me and said, "You thought it would be different, didn't you?"

"I guess I did."

"You thought maybe by shedding all that skin and cutting all those roots, you'd feel free."

"But all I feel is rootless."

"You thought that you could just throw away everything you didn't need."

"And all I feel is vulnerable."

"It gets better."

"I know. But I'm not as strong as you."

He laughed. "I'm not as strong as me, either."

That cracked me up.

"We walk," he said, "and it's not personal."

"But it's always personal," I said.

"Of course, it is," he said.

"When I was young I knew joy and it was something other than where I came from."

"And then you got older and found out that there was no joy worth having if it didn't include where you came from."

"Rabbi?"

"Yes?"

"I would miss you if you were gone."

"I'm never here."

"But I'm not alone."

"Just keep walking, pilgrim. Just keep walking."

"I can feel the joy of the man I'm going to become."

"Just keep walking. Just keep walking."

3

I was walking down the Plymouth Road and the Rabbi was there too. And I came upon a man who was carrying a load he couldn't bear or cast off. It seemed alive and changed shape with every step, as it undulated and heaved in his arms like the sea.

I thought I saw weasels, wolverines and badgers, vicious in panic, musky in distress, dart from the load and bite the man's cheek. I thought I saw warm kisses and soft lips, a sigh and a relenting.

My heart was full of pity and I wept for my brother.

"Why do you weep?" the Rabbi asked.

"Because my brother loves what he hates and hates what he loves."

"So is that why your face is bleeding?" the Rabbi asked.

"My face is bleeding because these tears turn to glass and they are sharp."

"The weasels, the wolverines and the badgers—they

are eating your face, aren't they?"

I cracked up, I couldn't help it, it was the way he said it.

"Yeah."

"And this is what you've lived your whole life longing for, isn't it?"

I nodded.

"Didn't I tell you to maintain your boundaries?"

He asked the question so tenderly. I choked up and fell into his arms, right there on the Plymouth Road, where they sell your eyes for a quarter and no man is ever sure of his companion.

"Trust me on this one, Pilgrim," he whispered, as I rested in his arms, "you can always find a face when you need one."

My ears bled at the touch of his breath on my neck.

"Thank you," I said.

"Don't mention it."

I carried my load down the Plymouth Road and the Rabbi was with me. We were smiling and for an instant it seemed to me as if we were both invisible.

And it was good.

We just walked awhile, me, the Rabbi and my brother, down the Plymouth Road, carrying our loads. And it was good.

•

I was walking down the Plymouth Road and the Rabbi was there too. And I saw my brother, but my brother was no different from me. He walked beside me and he walked in lock-step and he really kind of freaked me out. When I went up, he went up, and when I went down, he went down. Lock-step.

The first thing I thought when I saw my brother was that I didn't want to be tied down like that. You go up, you go down. But when you are up and they go down, it just really inhibits your mobility. The first thing they teach you in life-saving is how to break someone's arm, so the drowners don't, in a panic, take you down with them.

"What kind of stunt are you pulling here?" I asked the Rabbi.

"Get used to it, kid," he said, "you're going to need to walk blind and when you do, you're going to need your brother."

"But..."

"Don't be a fool, it's not like he trusts you either."

"I mean..."

"Don't even try, it's all about the rhythm and you've always known that."

"Doesn't mean I've always known how to keep the beat."

"Your brother is here. Why don't you just walk with him?"

"Like I have a choice!"

"Don't be petulant."

My brother sort of looked at me out the corner of his eye. I acknowledged his presence. He was kind of shy. We just walked awhile, me, my brother, and the Rabbi. I was intrigued.

Still, I was pissed, didn't want to meet the Rabbi's eye...

We just kept walking. Me and my brother and the Rabbi.

•

I was walking down the Plymouth Road with my brother and the Rabbi and I kept seeing artichoke hearts. All along the road there were artichoke hearts.

"Someone's had their leaves shorn," I said, "am I right?"

I looked at my brother and the Rabbi for some you-got-that-right-kid, but they just looked at me. There was an uncomfortable silence.

"I'm just saying, someone's going to have a rude awakening, someone's going to have to look in the mirror."

My brother and the Rabbi looked embarrassed.

"I'm not wearing any pants, am I?"

We just walked.

"Son of a bitch!"

"It's alright pilgrim," the Rabbi said, "happens to the best of us."

"You want I should take my pants off?" my brother asked, swallowing a laugh.

"I don't even like artichoke hearts," I said.

My brother and the Rabbi burst out laughing.

I was so pissed, but I was laughing too.

"What the hell?" I cried in mock outrage.

We laughed so hard my sides like to burst, artichoke hearts everywhere you looked.

•

The Devil Berates Pilgrim and Pilgrim Seduces the Devil

The devil said: You just keep flapping your gums. You just keep writing checks, but you got nothing in the bank.

I said: It all depends on what you mean by nothing.

He said: It's winners and losers in this world and there's no neutral ground.

I said: I've seen that movie and neither one of us were in it.

He said: You'll see, everyone pays in the end.

I said: I bought the ticket, I'll take the ride.

He said: You'll be sorry.

I said: Among other things.

Then I said: Have you lost weight? You look good.

He said: Well, I have been eating my vegetables.

I said: Whatever you're doing, keep doing it.

He said: I know what you're doing.

I said: I know, but we both know you can't resist it.

He said: You're little and I will devour you.

I said: I bet you could. You're so strong.

He said: I hate you.

I said: Did you know you're eyes are beautiful when you're mad?

•

When Mr. Bournesmith Finally Arrived

When Mr. Bournesmith finally arrived, his limousine having been detained on Route 1, he entered a local high school gymnasium in Central New Jersey and opened his mouth. There was a pep rally going on at the time, so the kids were pretty much savages to begin with. Whipped up. Loaded for bear. I mean, you just knew someone was going to have to pay.

He opened his mouth.

But before that, he started to grow, he just kept getting bigger, and he was pretty big to begin with. It started to get alarming. His body had always been plump and not just fat, but plump, like you wanted to get close, like there was ripeness and safety, if you could just burrow in, snuggle up—cling to his girth. But he just kept growing, until his girth smothered everything around it.

When Mr. Bournesmith finally arrived, bleachers were bull-dozed out of alignment as his belly advanced. There was a horrible sound of metal stretching as his thighs swelled. Backboards were shattering like heads through windshields. Kids were bursting like squeezed cherry tomatoes.

When Mr. Bournesmith finally arrived, blood squirted from ears and made squishing noises as Mr. Bournesmith's body expanded, bursting through jagged window panes, like water from a Fourth of July hose, with your thumb on the opening, maintaining the pressure, cold water running up your sleeve.

He opened his mouth.

Silly old Mr. Bournesmith, always getting himself into jams! Isn't that Mr. Bournesmith all over again? Always opening his mouth and swallowing his own ears?

•

Plymouth Road Memoir

What was maddening on the Plymouth Road was the constant awareness that, though the majority of pilgrims one met along the road shared your conviction that it was possible to become someone new, born again, etc., there was, nonetheless, a sizable minority that was struggling just as hard to hang on to who they always already were, or more exactly, to be anyone at all. For every two Huck Finns, there were was at least one Aunt Polly—and this was on the Plymouth Road, which anyone with any sense could see was, at best, a major thoroughfare among the backstreets, and hardly the main drag. It served as a reminder that the Pilgrim Road was important to you because it was slightly out of the way. It was celebrated because it was the road less travelled, and you loved it because just taking it made you feel different, unique, called.

It's no headline that the Plymouth Road never existed on any map, and when roads appeared that were given the name, they weren't the same road you found yourself walking. This often led to great confusion, but sometimes enlightenment, as well. Once along the road I saw a crossroads leading to the orchard, it turned out to be the exit ramp to Ann Arbor. Not a bad place to be, but hardly the place to which I was going.

The hard truth is that Huck was never welcome on Main Street, and the river just always rolled and never knew, or presumably cared, that it was named. If you were on the Plymouth Road, either you couldn't make it on Main Street, or you never could bring yourself to accept that Main Street was the only road to take, which pretty much amounted to the same thing.

The pilgrims on the Plymouth Road were all refugees, uprooted and displaced, the vast majority of which would have just stayed home if they could have, and yet, they just kept walking. Along the Plymouth Road. As if walking itself, leaving one's kindred, leaving one's land, going to a place to which I will show you, as if the sheer act of getting on board and needing no ticket were itself the fulfillment of a promise.

You met a lot of strange customers along the Plymouth Road, and you saw a lot of casualties along the way, and there were many nights you questioned your own judgment and longed for the cessation of the longing itself, but it wasn't like you didn't give thanks and rejoice with every step on the road, that narrow way, that royal road of dreams and faith.

That should be noted as well: the pilgrims who took to the Plymouth Road suffered the consequences of their choices, but at the same time received rare blessings and gifts, signs and portents of a time to come and a promised land—even discrete moments of ecstasy and release—that could never be found or savored on the main drag, though they only received those blessing and gifts in hardship and lack and squalor and in humiliation. The road isn't for everyone, but it is there for the ones who need it—and that's one of the greatest lessons of the road itself: gratitude.

I wouldn't have had it any other way, which is why I always did penance on the Plymouth Road, always paid my toll and peeled the onion—pay the man!—always and only finding the Rabbi outside the camp.

•

I was walking down the Plymouth Road; it was me, the Rabbi and my brother, and we came upon a man who operated the locks on some out of the way—some no-name—canal, feeding the system, the infrastructure—the Erie Canal. And he pulled the levers, and he turned the dials, and he opened gates and closed gates, and raised the water level, and lowered the water level, and his whole life he had allowed boats and barges to get to where they were going, and goods to where they were needed, and passage to some other place, some other place, just get me the fuck out of here, on all those last chance American boats, last chance American barges; but he'd never been to Buffalo, never himself, left his little station in Waterloo, NY—a way station, itself—a backwater, a becalming, not properly a part of the Erie Canal, though it could get you there, which was the point. The Great Lakes.

And this man had spent his whole life making it possible for other people to get to where they were going and goods to where they were needed, and he'd never been a damn place himself, just remained at his station, a secondary station, feeding into the Erie Canal, so that people and goods could get to where they were going, make passage, finally and reliably arrive, just that and nothing else. And it was so very long after the railroads, and so very long after the highway system, and so very long after Wall Street and anyone caring.

And I said to the man, this is what I said, "Don't you feel used?"

And he looked at me, he looked at me a long time, like he was perplexed, like he was hearing a language he used to speak, long ago, when he was young, long before the stars fell from the sky, fell from the sky like ripe figs, and the heavens rolled up like a scroll.

And he said, this is what he said to me, "Does the nail complain because it's not a hammer?"

And I said, this is what I said, "Yeah, it does. It most certainly does."

And he said, "I'm not a nail and neither are you."

And the Rabbi said nothing. And my brother said nothing. And I opened my mouth to say something, but I had nothing, and nothing came out. The canal man pulled his levers and twisted his dials, and boats and barges got to where they were going. The Great Lakes. The water flowed.

This hammer is so fricking heavy.

The canal man didn't look up when I waved goodbye. Everybody was going home. The Great Lakes.

•

I was walking down the Plymouth Road and I asked the Rabbi if it would get better.

I said, "It gets better, right?"

And he said, "Technically it's never been any worse or any better."

"Yeah, but it gets better right?"

"Your love has to grow bigger than your outrage."

"Oh for Christ's sake!"

"Language, pilgrim, language!"

"You probably think this is pretty funny, don't you?" I asked the Rabbi.

"Wouldn't you?" he asked in reply.

4

I was walking down the Plymouth Road and its edges were all bleeding over. Homeric shades from down in the hole were approaching me.

"Give us blood! Give us blood!", they were shrieking.

And then suddenly they would turn into some guy in McCaffrey's telling me about this week's sale on pork loins.

"It's a steal, dude."

It was unnerving, as if I could no longer manage the compartmentalizing of the two worlds, and a whole lot depended upon me keeping those two worlds straight.

The Rabbi was no where to be found. I was on my own. It was a real horror show.

Some lady named Berenice was trying to extract someone's teeth, and out on the docks they were doing things to Herman Melville that were unspeakable. I witnessed the dissection of Nathaniel Hawthorne by several farm families at the Mercer County Library, and it was all done in the dark. Afterwards, all the surgeons repaired to the traditional chicken pot pie dinner in Dutch Neck.

Ralph Waldo was there too, and his hair was on fire and he was laughing hysterically, and he was quoting Scripture, "When I am weak, then I am strong! When I am weak, then I am strong!" He was rubbing himself inappropriately in public and ruining his reputation.

Emerson on the Plymouth Road.

And yet, all the while, the other world—the straight world—was crashing in and everybody was mowing their lawns and attending travel soccer matches and murmuring under their breath. They landed a space shuttle on the Intrepid in New York.

I cried out in my anger and my shame, "I am leaving! I am leaving!", but it just turned out to be another Paul Simon song.

"Had enough?" the Rabbi asked.

"Where the hell were you!" I screamed, unsettled by the depth of my own rage, the cliffs of the palisades collapsing into the Hudson.

"Where I go, you cannot follow," he said.

"You left me alone!"

"That's not even the half of it, pilgrim."

"What do you expect of me?"

"Everything, and I'm not even here."

The erosion ceased, the world grew calm, suddenly nothing threatened on the Plymouth Road, and the levee stopped breaking—Washington crossed the Delaware. All things being equal, I just settled down.

Tending to the whiplash.

"You hungry?," the Rabbi asked. "I know a place down the road, they do a chicken francese that's to die for."

"They got fish and chips?"

"You know it son, they got fish."

"I'm so hungry, you think the levee's gonna hold?"

"Let's eat first and then see how we feel."

"I'm scared, Rabbi."

"This place I know, it's just around the bend. We're half-way there and back. We're practically there."

I kept walking, and I looked but the Rabbi was no-where to be found. The levee groaned. That's the way it was. Things kept going back and forth.

If you're hungry enough, you just keep walking, past the country clubs—alone, but not alone—past the full scale invasions of column upon column of desire—with and without the Rabbi—who is always there, if not here—past the haunted mansions on the hill, past the subdivisions, past the howling banshees of loneliness in the heart of America—past the night-time-illuminated baseball diamonds, where all the pale ghosts demand their black blood behind home plate—past the bones of the pilgrims mouldering in patriot graves on Bunker Hill and Haymarket Square, you just...around the bend, just around the bend...keep walking—with the crash on the levee always about to begin—and the smell of bombs—you just keep walking.

"What's it going to be, pilgrim, the Chicken or the Fish?" the Rabbi asked, as the membrane melted and solidified—and the heavens forever threatened rain and you were not erased in the ambiguity.

"What's it going to be?"

As if maybe it was about time to get off the Plymouth Road and set some roots somewhere.

•

The Confidence Man Explains the Long Con

God is always in the room you don't want to go into. He's waiting there for you. And you never want to open that door. All the pikers and hanger-ons, all the flim flam boys and faro dealers, they are always just going to give you permission to stay where you are, selling you the license to never open that door. They are selling you real estate you already own. They are collecting rent on your shackles. And most of the time you're happy to pay. Doesn't that beat all? We are all too happy to pay to avoid being who we are.

OK. Maybe calling it God is the problem. The scandal of particularity. It doesn't really matter what you call it. It's not like the atheist is ever going to avoid having to open that door. It's not like the door wouldn't be there, just waiting to be opened, if there weren't no God. What, do we have to speak baby-talk? God is never what we mean when we say "God". Duh! Jeeze Louise. Anyone who has ever felt awe knows that. Anyone who has ever loved and lost and lived to tell the tale knows that. You can't reduce these things to names. You can't tame the tempest in words.

For all intents and purposes, there's nothing but the door and the room you don't want to enter. And here's the thing, boys: It is all too easy to label what lies beyond the door, in the room we don't want to enter, evil. It's red meat to politicians, and priests, ministers and clergy, the numbers runners of our body politic. They got ways to make you turn your cowardice into virtue every which way to Sunday.

You got pulpit-pounders and shamans, tarot card readers to the stars, you got prognosticators and mediums who channel the wisdom of lost masters in Atlantis. You got puritan divines and catholic prelates. You got skeptics and debunkers, devotees of the cult of reason, you got professors and auto-didactics, you got the three card monte boys in Times Square and roulette dealers in Monte Carlo.

You got every thing you need to justify not opening that damned door.

Jeeze Louise. It's not like you don't have to open it. I mean, it's not like it won't ever stop being there just waiting for you to open it. It's not like you don't have to take your own bath.

So what are you waiting for? Just open the damn door. Whatever is there waiting for you, knows your true name. It's been waiting for you forever.

•

I was walking down the Plymouth Road and I was pretty much done with it. I didn't want to play hide and seek anymore. I didn't want to be away from my family.

I had Mongo Santamaria playing in my earphones and visions I just couldn't use anymore. I was digging a hole to find the place where revelation met imagination and everything around me just kept affirming my suspicion that you can't dig your way out of that hole.

Sooner or later you're going to have to hoist your

own damn sail and trust in the wind.

I had lunch with Woodsworth and Coleridge. They turned out to be a couple of guys with their own responsibilities. It wasn't like they were going to ever help you move, even if you rented the van and promised them pizza.

It was the same with Paul Ricoeur and Arthur Rimbaud and Hank Williams. Walt Whitman was dead and Jack Kerouac was still blowing—blowing a cool wind all the way from Baudelaire to Edgar Allan Poe, to Charlie Parker—but the clock was ticking and it wasn't like I was getting any younger.

I am not anywhere other than where I have always already exhausted my entire life in struggling to arrive. And maybe it's time to just be here.

I want to build something. I ain't no anarchist.

"You think you're ready?" the Rabbi asked.

"Not really," I replied.

"Lo, I am with you until the end of the age."

"That's funny because it's true and not true all at the same time."

"I never promised you a rose garden."

"You're just a laugh riot, aren't you?"

"As long as you keep laughing."

"Yeah. As long as I keep laughing."

No one said nothing.

"I'm scared, Rabbi."

"I'd be worried about you if you weren't."

"I'm just working on a building."

"A Holy Ghost building."

"Thank you."

"See you in your dreams, pilgrim."

'Yeah. See you."

Morning dawned on Mercer County in Central New Jersey like it had been planned or something.

CPSIA information can be obtained at www.ICGtesting.com
Printed in the USA
BVOW03s2131071113

335677BV00002B/5/P

9 781937 402433